W9-BOL-162

BY THE SAME AUTHOR

IRELAND
MINISTER FOR JUSTICE
THE LAMBERT REVELS
THE DISTANCE AND
THE DARK
THE ANGLO-IRISH
MY NAME IS NORVAL

JOHNNIE CROSS

A NOVEL

by

TERENCE de VERE WHITE

ST MARTIN'S PRESS

NEW YORK

Library of congress Catalog Card Number 83-50468

ISBN 0-312-44463-X

First published in Great Britain by
Victor Gollancz Ltd
First U.S. Edition
10 9 8 7 6 5 4 3 2 1

For
Charlotte and Colin Franklin

NOTE

The novelist George Eliot was born Mary Anne Evans on 22 November 1819. In 1854 she set up house with George Henry Lewes, a married man. Lewes died on 28 November 1878. On 6 May 1880 George Eliot married John Walter Cross. She died on 22 December of the same year.

In 1885 Cross published his *Life of George Eliot as related in her Letters and Journals* in three volumes. He died on 2 November 1924.

The authoritative biography of George Eliot has been written by Gordon S. Haight, who has also edited her letters in nine volumes. The present writer wishes to thank Miss Elizabeth Hall for access to Cross family letters — which were not, as my story suggests, left on a bus in 1924.

T. de V. W.

OVERTURE

Colin

I NEVER EXPECTED anything from my Venice book; it was written in a hurry and would not have been written at all if my publisher had given me any encouragement when I told him about my novel. 'It is impossible to sell first novels at the present time', he assured me, and then, to avert the danger, I suppose, 'Why don't you write a book about Venice? There hasn't been one since E.V. Lucas's and things must have changed there since the War. The Lido — the drabbest strip of beach in Europe — is swarming with Americans. I'm sure they would like something to read between cocktails and adultery. Fill it up with droppable names. We can be lavish with illustrations. I think you should have a go.'

Laura was quite enthusiastic about the project when I rang her up in Edinburgh. The idea of my trying my hand at a novel hadn't appealed to her at all; to the Scots mind a man engaged to be married should get down to a solid job and put dreams of glory behind him. I wanted her to come to Venice while I was doing my homework, but her grim parents put their hooves down, and she did what she was told. They don't approve of me, I fear, and have warned their daughter against journalists as a species. Has no-one told them that this is 1923? John Knox is dead a long time. But I couldn't persuade her.

I stayed at the Casa Frollo on the Giudecca for six months, and returned with a draft that I licked into shape in six weeks. ('You didn't waste any time. You had no distractions; but I did miss you terribly.' And I missed her.) It wasn't as if I was already in love with the place, as I should have been when I dared to write about it. I had never been there before. My instinct to get Laura to come with me was, I am now convinced, as much for the book's sake as for mine. They gave it a fetching cover and rather sophisticated illustrations, and I dropped every name I could find from bloody Byron to windy James, as I burbled on about literary associations. The whole, as you can see, aimed at readers of *Vogue*. At that level it served a purpose: giving up-to-date information about tourist requirements, but in every other respect it was born dead. I gave the reason why in the introduction.

Venice is not so much a city as a back-drop for an opera that was never performed. Mozart could have written the music; Wagner would have wanted to, but he made the wrong sort of noise; it wouldn't have fitted in with the frivolity of the baroque, the worldliness of the large churches, the preciousness of the little ones, the sugar cake that the Doge's palace is, the Ali Baba interior of St. Mark's, and all those bottoms and bosoms Tiepolo sprinkled so profusely over his ceilings. Nowhere, except in France, do the fronts of houses tell us so little about what is going on behind them. As you chug down the Grand Canal you get a deserted impression of absent owners and empty rooms. For these reasons you must never go to Venice without a companion, and your companion must be someone with whom you are in love.

That was the bit that was quoted in reviews, of which there were more than I had expected. (It must have been a lean week for literary editors.) Of course I was delighted — so was the publisher — but when I saw the attention that little bastard of a book was getting, I sighed, thinking of my four brain-children on whom so much loving care had been lavished, and no-one took any notice (this was my fifth book).The happy ending of the story was a review by Gosse in his *Sunday Times* column. I stared at it in amazement and at my name in that place; euphoria evaporated somewhat when I found that I was being used to launch an appeal for the revival of Howells, the novelist who for years was American consul in Venice. My book was mentioned only in the first and last lines of the review, but unexceptionably, and I felt that morning the glow of celebrity.Never in my life had I bought so many copies of a newspaper; at twopence it seemed excellent value.

I

Colin

I COULDN'T HELP but notice a subtle change in the atmosphere when I came into the club, among the older members particularly. They belonged to two species, watch dog and lap dog. Perhaps I imagined it, the change may have only been in myself — greater confidence; but I had the impression that when I passed where they were lurking the watch dogs looked as if they had reached an agreement that the calves of my legs should be issued a safe conduct, and the lap dogs could almost be seen to wag their tails.

There was one of the latter whose manner had been propitiatory from the start — the oldest member, I guessed. He fell asleep after lunch every day in his armchair — he always sat in the same one — and it was fascinating in its melancholy way to watch the ritual that attended this retreat from the world: the eyes behind the gold spectacles glazed over imperceptibly under cover of short fits of furious concentration on his newspaper; then the head fell forward like a railway signal; with that one half of the *Financial Times* collapsed on the carpet; flaccid fingers still held the other; gradually the mouth opened; and now sweet peace had descended, witnessed by a steady susurration; sudden starts were followed by violent commotion as if a collision had taken place in the nasal passages. Then peace again.

A hideous shudder preceded the awakening, followed by a vigorous dog act, shaking off the waters of his dream. Then he looked round cautiously, and snapped the newspaper up. If he caught my eye he smiled to assure me that whatever impression I might have formed to the contrary, he had not been asleep. I smiled back, but not always as warmly as I was invited to. He would have liked to exchange a few words for reassurance, and left it to me to begin, but I could think of nothing to say, and I rather dreaded establishing a precedent. To make up for this, if we met when we were both on the move, we greeted each other like old friends — old friends in a hurry.

On this particular day I had called on my publisher on my way to lunch, coming into his office like a conquering hero, leaving it with my conceit in disarray; notwithstanding the nice things the critics had said, the public had shown uncommendable restraint in the book shops. My elderly friend either lunched very early or not at all because he was always in his chair when I came into the smoking room. He was there today, but instead of the usual nod followed by instant retreat behind the newspaper, he struggled to his feet and came across the room to where I was sitting. It cost him an effort, that was plain. On his legs at last, he pulled himself up to his full height, seemingly about a foot taller than the old man I so often passed on the stairs. He stood in front of my chair and beamed down on me.

'I must congratulate you, Cathcart, on the very favourable notices your book is getting. I sent a note to Mr Wilson at Bumpus's to keep me a copy. Anything to do with Venice has a peculiar attraction for me. I was particulary delighted to see my old friend Gosse's favourable attention in the *Sunday Times*. He, of course, would have picked up the literary references. The book is studded with them, I gather. Why, I am curious to know, no mention of George Eliot?'

'I must admit that I never associated *her* with Venice.'

'Oh, dear me. Yes. She was lyrical about its attractions.'

'What a pity we didn't have this talk when I was writing the book. You would have saved me from a gaffe.' (I wasn't much worried. I was playing up to the old boy.)

'Yes, indeed, but you might like to make good the omission in future editions. I'd be only too pleased if I could be of any service.'

The last sentence was accompanied by a gentle lowering of himself beside me on to the sofa, in the manner of a crane releasing its burden into the hold of a ship. It would be the devil getting himself up, but there was a quiet purposefulness about his proceeding that held no prospect of this taking place in the immediate future. He had come on a visit. The threat of boredom loomed large, but the old man had made a noble effort to be civil, and I was not so used to attention to have become blasé. I lapped it up.

He was a very well-looked-after old gentleman, smelling of expensive soap, with skin the colour and texture of Fortnum and Mason's meringue cases; what was left of his hair was fine silk. I saw what he must have looked like as a baby. There was nothing to be done for the rheumy eyes but dab them occasionally with his handkerchief, the size of a table napkin. I tried, before he told me about himself, to place him, and decided that he had been a house-master at one of the older public schools who, through his wife, had come in for a small sum of capital. Its daily movements were the chief interest and concern of his retirement.

'Yes,' he said, breathing stertorously, 'you must be the man I've been waiting for; someone will have to stop the rot. The War is made the scapegoat, but it had seeped in before that. Shaw, Wells — all that crew — were cocking snooks at every tradition of decency long before the War. But this man Strachey has put them in the shade, and one might have expected better from him. The Stracheys after all . . . I am sorry for the family; they can't like it. All that sneery suggestiveness — so unmanly. *Eminent Victorians* — they *were* eminent. He is a skunk trying to pull them down. I could forgive him Manning, Arnold even, but, dammit, Gordon was a hero, and it's when he libels Miss Nightingale that I get really angry. What that woman accomplished . . . Think of it. When I do, I long to thrash him. How George Eliot would have hated it.

'I don't go to the theatre nowadays — my ears — but they tell me things there are quite as bad . . . Coward . . . a cockney youth . . . outrageous. We are back at the Restoration, but with what a crew! Where is it all going to end? Between ourselves, there was always a certain amount of looking the other way — you know what I mean. One picked up the knack — women did instinctively — and a great deal of embarrassment and bad blood was avoided. Of course it required an effort, but everyone knew the rules of the game. Life was less sophisticated in America, where I spent most of my time as a very young man — left school early, Father died. I knew the America of the Pilgrim Fathers tradition. Very little of *that* left. More's the pity. But why am I going on like this? Forgive me. I came over to talk to you about your book.'

There was a look in his eye that told me he was lying. My book was an excuse to exercise one of the bees in his bonnet. I recognized the symptoms from an old lady I knew who thinks about nothing else nowadays but the danger of tinned salmon. In her proselytizing zeal she will simulate an interest in any topic, biding her time before she moves in for the kill. I was in for a lecture — that was all too clear. I would give him the floor until quarter to three, allow five minutes for disentanglement, then rush off for an appointment with my dentist.

'They do it to attract attention to themselves, and they are encouraged to in the belief that indecency is good for sales — the most insidious kind of prostitution. I am quite certain that a book can be successful with the public without appealing to the dirty dog in human nature. From what I read in the notices of your book, your writing is celebratory. You have not been infected by this debunking bug. There is room for a book like yours, pointing out what a priceless asset we have here in England in our villages. Soon it will be too late; we must preserve what is left of traditional life. Pump money into the C of E, I say. Make it worth while for the best type of young man to put on the dog-collar. There must be some left who can think of better ways of spending Sunday than taking flappers round the country on the backs of motor-bikes. What's wrong with Australia? Can't we subsidize emigration of ex-servicemen and their families? All that empty country. Wouldn't fancy it at all myself. I ask these questions. You mustn't pay too much attention to me. I'm an old man.'

'You should write to *The Times*.'

'I have, in my day, but only on my proper topics. My main concern is investment growth. At a time of panic in the City I wrote, "Our hardiest war chest is our holding of American securities". I hope the message was taken note of at the time.'

I looked suitably impressed, but I thought we had wandered very far from my book, moreover I got the impression that his nerve was failing him; he was holding back the real purpose of his raid. He said something. I wasn't listening, but I nodded, pretending I had heard. We stared in front of us like people watching a funeral pass by. Then he looked hard at me. I suppose he was trying to measure me before he committed himself.

'What was it you said you were working on at present? My memory is so bad I can't keep anything in my head.'

I hadn't said, but still . . . 'My publisher wants me to write a book about India — I lived there as a child — but I am not very keen myself on the idea at the moment. I don't want to go abroad for the length of time it would require.'

He was not paying any attention to me. Whatever was his equivalent to my old lady's tinned salmon was kicking inside him to get out. He wouldn't be able to keep it in much longer. It came at last.

'I may have the very book for you. Reading Gosse on Sunday, I said to myself, "There's my man." It was quite a coincidence, because I put the idea up to Gosse years ago when he made such a hit with *Father and Son*. "Edmund," I said, "I believe I have the subject for your next book, but you won't be able to publish it until I'm dead." "I am very much obliged to you," he replied, "but unless you can guarantee that sad event will take place reasonably soon I have more pressing demands on the short time that is left to *me*." A supercilious fellow, Gosse, I've known him for a long time; but he did have a point. I'm still in circulation, and that was more than ten years ago. You won't have so long to wait. Once a man gets to eighty-four every knock on the door sounds as if it were for him.'

This note struck me as the one to escape on. I took a covert glance at my watch.

'This has been very pleasant, but I must be off. My dentist wont't wait if I'm late for my appointment.'

I had very little compunction. If I didn't extricate myself we would be there for the afternoon, and I had given him quite a good hearing. So I was unprepared for the stricken look on his old crumpled face. Again he brought to mind a baby, a most unhappy, a sadly disappointed baby.

'Dentists are busy men.' He conceded that. If he was a stock club bore he would have then begun about his own, but he refrained, or didn't want to; he had something else he was beseeching me to let him tell, and I knew it would be cruel to leave him with the *Financial Times* without something else to look forward to.

'Why do we not lunch here together some day? I would like to talk about the book.'

'Would you really? But what a delightful *suggestion*.'

His relief was unconcealed; his eagerness shameless. I cut in before the 'Why not tomorrow?' that was observable on the tip of his tongue slipped out. 'Let me look in my diary. What's wrong with Monday?'

Some relic of old decency made him pull out his. Even from where I stood I could see the virgin page. 'Monday looks all right to me,' he said.

'Let's meet here then, a little before one. I shall look forward to that.'

As I made my escape, I thought I saw interested eyes watching me (I am such a *very* new member) and on the stairs another old boy who had never spoken to me before smiled conspiratorially. 'I saw you talking to George Eliot's widow.'

I thought of George Eliot as long buried and very dead. She seemed remoter than Dickens, and my efforts to read her had always ended in a scoreless draw — except for *Middlemarch*. That I enjoyed thoroughly, and was so much impressed that I went back and tried one of the others, but soon got bogged down again. I am a journalist, not a man of letters — how pretentious that sounds! What I meant to say was that in my experience the sort of person who had read everything and can place writers neatly in their right compartments is not always adept at pushing a pen himself when the opportunity arrives. This is by way of excuse for my complete incredulity. In the taxi I pinched myself; was it all a day dream? Would I soon wake up?

My dentist was delighted with the incident. He, it turns out, is a George Eliot fan, and he whistled when I told him the bit about 'the widow'.

'I suppose he could be still alive. Let me see. She died somewhere around 1880, and they had only been married a very short time, less than a year. His name was Croker, was it? That doesn't sound right. *Cross*. That's it. She married this Cross man who was years and years younger than she was. A curate, I seem to remember. Suppose she was sixty at the time and he about a quarter of a century younger, he wouldn't be much more than eighty now. So, it is quite possible. I say, how exciting for you.'

The drill was in my mouth, and I could only listen and feel ashamed. The prospect even now did not seem *exciting*. That was not the word I would have leaped at, but certainly it did give much more point to the next encounter. After all it was not every day one had such an opportunity. If only it had been Charlotte Brontë's husband or a brother even of Jane Austen (but that was going back a little); almost *any* writer would be more alluring than that great horse-faced woman. How had he brought himself to *do* it?

'He isn't a clergyman,' I said.

'That makes it all the better.'

'I'll tell you what happens on my next visit, but I hope that won't be for ages.'

It is very helpful having a literary dentist. Mine had alerted me to the necessity of doing some homework before Monday's encounter. I decided to go at once — the afternoon was already in such disarray — and do some research in the London Library.

I looked there in the current *Who's Who* but could not find my man. This made me sceptical. If one didn't get into *Who's Who* for marrying George Eliot — it deserved the Victoria Cross — what was the qualification? I went up to the biography section. The George Eliot shelf had the appearance of not having been disturbed for quite some time. It was dominated by two sets in three volumes of her *Life* by J.W. Cross. I read 'Cross' twice before it sank in. I had been talking to the horse and now here was his mouth. I leaped into it. This was not, judging by the date on the ticket, its usual experience. Two years had passed since the *Life* last came down for an airing.

The plan of the biography was artless, a few recollections of her in early days, but for the most part, a sequence of her letters and diary entries with the date and the name of the correspondent in the margin. It was evident that much cutting had been done, Mr Cross had been self-effacing in the extreme. When he did obtrude himself to comment or help the reader with supplementary detail his identity merged almost completely in the text; the narrow margin of indentation was deliberate. I skimmed and skipped through volumes one and two, and only settled down when my friend made his appearance in Rome in 1860. He was there on holiday with his mother and sister.

'It was during this journey that I, for the first time, saw my future wife at Rome. My eldest sister had married Mr W.H. Bullock (now Mr W. H. Hall), of Six-Mile Bottom, Cambridgeshire, and they were on their wedding journey at Rome, when they happened to meet Mr and Mrs Lewes by chance in the Pamfili Doria Gardens. They saw a good deal of one another, and when I arrived with my mother and another sister, we went by invitation to call at the Hotel Minerva, where Mr Lewes had found rooms on their first arrival in Rome. I have a very vivid recollection of George Eliot sitting on a sofa with my mother by her side, entirely engrossed with her. Mr Lewes entertained my sister and me on the other side of the room. But I was very anxious to hear also the conversation on the sofa, as I was better acquainted with George Eliot's books than with any other literature. And through the dimness of these fifteen years, and all that has happened in them, I still seem to hear, as I first heard them, the low, earnest, deep musical tones of her voice: I still seem to see the fine brows, with the abundant auburn-brown hair framing them, the long head broadening at the back, the grey-blue eyes, constantly changing in expression, but always with a very loving, almost deprecating, look at my mother, the finely-formed, thin, transparent hands . . .'

Next day the Leweses went on to Assisi, the Crosses to Naples. They were to meet again in the autumn when the Leweses visited the Crosses at Weybridge.

George Eliot makes this entry in her diary for 31st August 1869.

'*We went to Weybridge, walked on St. George's Hill and lunched with Mrs Cross and her family.*'

Then Cross took over: 'This visit to Weybridge is a very memorable one to me, because there my own first intimacy with George Eliot began, and the bonds with my family were knitted very much closer. Mr and Mrs Bullock were staying with us; and my sister, who had some gift for music, had set one or two of the songs from "The Spanish Gypsy". She sang one of them — "On through the woods, the pillared pines," — and it affected George Eliot deeply. She moved quickly to the piano, and kissed Mrs Bullock very warmly in her tears. Mr and Mrs Lewes were in deep trouble, owing to the illness of Thornton Lewes; we were also in much anxiety as to the approaching confinement of my sister with her first child; and I was on the eve of departure for America. Sympathetic feelings were strong enough to overlap the barrier (often hard to pass) which separates acquaintanceship from friendship. A day did the work of years. Our visitors had come to the house as acquaintances, they left it as lifelong friends. And the sequel of that day greatly intensified the intimacy.'

Now back in England for keeps, Cross begins to appear regularly in G.E.'s Journal. He is 'nephew Johnnie', advising on investments, planning excursions, looking out for houses in the country for the Leweses, introducing them to the delights of the new game of lawn tennis, which has been putting croquet completely in the shade. Tired, ill, stiff, often in pain — the tale is a litany of physical ills — the old couple are insatiable. When weather keeps them in, Cross sets up badminton in the so-expensively decorated drawing room of the Pines (near Regent's Park). Cross is an athletic fellow, for ever rowing or going on mountain-climbing expeditions.

November 28th 1878 Lewes dies. Cross leaves his mother's death-bed to be at his side. The aftermath is in the Queen-Victoria-mourning-for-Albert tradition. The disconsolate widow shuts the world out, lives in her darling dead one's private room, immersed in his papers. All work of her own must be put aside while she completes his last book *Problems of Life and Mind*; and the only communications she makes with the outside world are in connection with a studentship that she has decided to set up in his memory. Cross was called in on this, but I found the details less than deeply interesting. My eyes were glued to the margins.

Letter to J.W. Cross 22 Jan 1879. '*Some time if I live, I shall be able to see you — perhaps sooner than anyone else — but not yet. Life seems to get harder instead of easier.*'

This is followed by a letter to J.W. Cross, 30 Jan 1879. '*When I said "some time" I meant still a distant time. I want to live a little time that I may do certain things for his sake. So I try to keep up my strength, and I work as much as I can to save my mind from imbecility. But that is all at present. I can go through anything that is mere business. But what used to be joy is joy no longer, and what is pain is easier because he has not to bear it.*'

Never had I encountered such a history of illness as in the Lewes family. The Pines must have been like a nursing home. When George Eliot wasn't prostrated with sickness, Lewes was; and sometimes they both were. How did they write so much? Travel abroad? Go to theatres, galleries, concerts, opera? Entertain? (The list of Sunday callers was like a random sample of the *Dictionary of National Biography*.)

On 7 Feb 1879, another letter to Cross. '*I do need your affection. Every sign of care for me from the beings I respect and love, is a help to me. In a week or two I think I shall want to see you. Sometimes, even now, I have a longing, but it is immediately counteracted by a fear. The perpetual mourner — the grief that can never be healed — is innocently enough felt to be wearisome by the rest of the world. And my sense of desolation increases. Each day seems to be a new beginning — a new acquaintance with grief.*'

Next day. '*If you happen to be at liberty to-morrow, or the following Friday, or to-morrow week, I hope I shall be well enough to see you. Let me know which day.*'

Johnnie called next day and, apparently, invited George Eliot to come and stay — he lived with a brother, Willie, and their unmarried sisters at Weybridge. The invitation was turned down; She couldn't leave home, She said, for the next two months. Two months pass. Then I found this:

'*I am in dreadful need of your counsel. Pray come to me when you can — morning, afternoon or evening.*' What was her dreadful need? We are not told, but Cross must have risen to the occasion because in the next paragraph he makes one of his rare self-projected appearances on the scene.

'From this time forward I saw George Eliot constantly. My mother had died in the beginning of the previous December — a week after Mr Lewes; and as my life had been very much bound up with hers, I was trying to find some fresh interest in taking up a new pursuit. Knowing very little Italian, I began Dante's *Inferno* with Carlyle's translation. The first time I saw George Eliot afterwards, she asked me what I was doing, and, when I told her, exclaimed, "Oh, I must read that with you." And so it was . . . not in a *dilettante* way, but with minute and careful examination of the construction of every sentence. The prodigious stimulus of such a teacher *(cotanto maestro)* made the reading a real labour of love. Her sympathetic delight in stimulating my newly awakened enthusiasm for Dante, did something to distract her mind from sorrowful memories.

'The divine poet took us into a new world. It was a renovation of life. At the end of May I induced her to play on the piano at

Witley for the first time: and she played regularly after that whenever I was there, which was generally once or twice a week, as I was living at Weybridge, within easy distance.

'Besides Dante, we read at this time a great many of Sainte-Beuve's *Causeries*, and much of Shakespeare and Wordsworth.'

I tried to picture the life of a man of forty who, when his mother dies, takes up learning Italian as a 'fresh interest', but my imagination wasn't up to it. I had noticed from occasional references in the text that George Eliot's choice of reading matter might have posed a challenge even to a polymath, and as she counted reading aloud as one of the pleasures of matrimony I wondered how Cross felt about it when his turn came. Looking back he might well have asked himself whether it was not to make up for times spent with Mother that he turned to Dante so much as preparing himself for what was in store. I glanced at her reading list of August 1868.

'Reading 1st Book of Lucretius, 6th Book of the *Iliad*, *Samson Agonistes*, Warton's *History of English poetry*, Grote, 2nd Volume, Marcus Aurelius, *Vita Nuova*, Vol. 4 Chap. 1 of the *Politique Positive*, Guest on *English Rhythms*, Maurice's *Lectures on Casuistry*.' Cross, presumably, had advance notice of what he was in for.

Towards the end of May George Eliot moved to Witley where 'nephew Johnnie' had found the Leweses a house. It was not far from Weybridge.

Johnnie played with his cards very close to his chest. We hear of him obliquely . . . once. George Eliot is writing to Mrs Burne-Jones. 'Thank you, dear, for caring whether I have any human angels to guard me. None are permanently here except my servants, but Sir James Paget has been down to see me, I have a very comfortable country practitioner to watch over me from day to day, and there is a devoted friend who is backwards and forwards continually to see that I lack nothing.'

Did Mrs Burne-Jones smell a rat? There was nothing to suggest the sex of the devoted friend, but that might in itself have been suggestive. I had already got an impression of a long following of 'devoted' women (Mrs Burne-Jones among them). Only a few days before she received that letter one had gone from Madame Bodichon to Miss Bonham-Carter. 'I spent an hour with Marian [George Eliot]. She was more delighted than I can say, and left me in good spirits for her — though she is wretchedly thin, and looks in her long, loose black dress like the black shadow of herself. She said she has so much to do that she must keep well — "the world was so *intensely interesting*". She said she would come next year to see me. We both agreed in the great love we had for life. In fact I think she will do more for us than ever.'

There is a hint of a sorority in that 'us', a college from which men are excluded. George Eliot might have felt she was letting down her admirers by letting a man play a comforting role when there were so many women on call. I tried to make a list of them, but decided to postpone the operation until I knew a little more. One peculiar result of this investigation was that I could not connect in my mind the elusive J.W. Cross who was responsible for this odd compilation and my anxious old friend on our club sofa.

There was less than a year to go before the marriage. I turned page after page, but except that one reference to the 'devoted friend', the bridegroom-to-be is not mentioned until immediately following a letter to Mrs Burne-Jones — 'Life has seemed worse without my glimpses of you' — Cross suddenly takes over.

'As the year went on, George Eliot began to see all her old friends again. But her life was nevertheless a life of heart-loneliness. Accustomed as she had been for so many years to solitude *à deux*, the want of close companionship continued to be very bitterly felt. She was in the habit of going with me very frequently to the National Gallery, and to South Kensington. This constant association engrossed me completely, and was a new interest to her. A bond of mutual dependence had been formed between us. On the 28th March she came down to Weybridge, and stayed till the 30th; and on the 9th April it was finally decided that our marriage should take place as soon, and as privately, as might be found practicable.'

As I read Cross's brief explanation over and over, I conjured up in my mind this pair, the banker and club man of forty with the plain, great-faced celebrity of sixty on his arm; he in the height of men's fashion, she in widow's weeds. At art exhibitions, concerts, and all the rest of it, she had fallen into Mother's place so far as he was concerned, and he may have felt a certain pride as the escort of the lady whom Sir James Paget, the Queen's surgeon, had described as 'the greatest genius — male or female — that we can boast of.' I got the impression that Johnnie's sisters basked in their brother's reflected glory. I know of several rich old ladies, widows for the most part, who have their Johnnie Crosses, but are not for the most part married to them, nor are the Johnnies usually of the marrying sort. They have nice little flats of their own somewhere, and come on long visits and go abroad with their George Eliots. The arrangement suits everyone. Johnnies tend to have the feline virtues; they are sleek and companionable and haven't to be put out at night. The ladies, always older than the Johnnies, prefer their house-trained ways to the unpredictable behaviour of the un-neutered cat.

I saw letters from George Eliot on the next few pages and halted speculation until I had examined these.

5th May 1880. 'I have something to tell you,' George Eliot writes to her friend Barbara Bodichon, 'which will doubtless be a great surprise to you; but since I have found that other friends, less acquainted with me and my life than you are, have given me their sympathy, I think that I can count on yours. I am going to do what not very long ago I should myself have pronounced impossible for me, and therefore I should not wonder if anyone else found my action incomprehensible.

'By the time you receive this letter I shall (so far as the future can be matter of assertion) have been married to Mr J.W. Cross, who, you know, is a friend of years, a friend much loved and trusted by Mr Lewes, and who, now that I am alone, sees his happiness in the dedication of his life to me . . . Mr Cross has taken the lease of a house, No. 4 Cheyne Walk, Chelsea, where we shall spend the winter and early spring, making Witley our summer home.'

Madame Bodichon did not receive the letter before she read in the newspapers for May 7th that George Eliot had married Cross at St. George's Hanover Square on the previous day. She was generous and wrote at once to wish her well. George Eliot replied from Verona.

'Charles says that my friends are chiefly hurt because I did not tell them of the approaching change in my life. But I really did not finally, absolutely decide — until only a fortnight before the event took place, so that at last everything was done in the utmost haste. However, there were four or five friends, of whom you were one, to whom I was resolved to write, so that they should at least get my letter on the morning of the 6th.

'I had more than once said to Mr Cross that you were that one of my friends who required the least explanation on the subject — who would spontaneously understand our marriage. . . .

'His family welcome me with the uttermost tenderness. All this is wonderful blessing falling to me beyond my share, after I had thought that my life was ended, and that, so to speak, my coffin was ready for me in the next room. Deep down below there is a hidden river of sadness, but this must always be with those who have lived long — and I am able to enjoy my newly reopened life. I shall be a better, more loving creature than I could have been in solitude. To be constantly, lovingly grateful for the gift of a perfect love, is the best illumination of one's mind to all the possible good there may be in store for man on this troublous little planet. . . .'

At this point I decided that I must take a day off for research before I met Cross again. I had begun by humouring him as the resident club bore, not suspecting that he had anything to tell me that I hadn't heard hundreds of times from others of that well-preserved species. But now I was intensely curious about him. There must be a story there, and the better-briefed I was when I met him the more likely I was to gain his confidence. I took out all three volumes of the first edition of his *Life* of George Eliot, uttering a silent prayer as I lifted them off the shelves that the librarian would ask no awkward questions about the amount of the library's collection that was lying about at home.

I settled in to the task after supper. First of all, what could I find out about the 'two or three persons' She had let into the secret of her coming wedding, apart from Barbara Bodichon and Mrs Congreve who She (whenever I called George Eliot 'she' I wrote it in my mind with a capital S) seemed to think was unlikely to take kindly to the news. Mrs Congreve is informed that 'a great momentous change is going to take place in my life. My indisposition last week, and several other subsequent circumstances, have hindered me from communicating it to you, and the time has been but short since the decision was come to. But with your permission Charles will call on you and tell you what he can on Saturday.' (Who the devil was Charles? I pushed on without checking the index.)

May 6th. *Married this day at 10.15 to John Walter Cross at St. George's Hanover Square. Present, Charles who gave me away, Mr and Mrs Druce, Mr Hall, William, Mary, Eleanor and Florence Cross. We went back to the Priory where we signed our wills. Then we started for Dover, and arrived there a little after five o'clock.*

With the aid of the index I was able to identify everyone mentioned as members of the Cross family. None of hers graced the ceremony. The ubiquitous Charles was, I discovered, Lewes's son. He had been saddled with the task of making her excuses to the close women friends She had kept in the dark. I didn't envy him his job. When his father died Charles had moved in to deal with the mail while George Eliot locked herself into the dead man's room to go through his papers and journals, with intervals of reading *In Memoriam*, which can have done nothing to lift her depression.

In the references to Charles I thought I caught a note of condescension, as if She didn't reckon him. He was used as a dogsbody, and as he didn't complain was supposed to like it and to resent the idea of anyone else being asked to help him with the dirty work. He had a wife and children, and must have missed their company. Charles, I felt, was hard-done-by. But I couldn't waste time on him; I wanted to see what happened on the honeymoon.

When at home She had a doctor in almost daily attendance, how was She going to get on without one on her travels? A letter was awaiting them in Paris from sister Eleanor. She was the first to hear about their journey. Not a word about pains or aches.

'Your letter was a sweet greeting to us on our arrival here yesterday. We had a millennial cabin on the deck of the Calais-Douvres, and floated over the Strait as easily as the saints float upward to heaven (in the pictures). At Amiens we were very comfortably housed, and paid two enraptured visits, evening and morning, to the Cathedral. I was delighted with J.'s delight in it. And we read our dear old cantos of the *Inferno* that we were reading a year ago, declining afterwards on *Eugénie Grandet*. The nice woman who waited on us made herself very memorable to me by her sketch of her own life. She went to England when she was nineteen as a lady's maid — had been much *ennuyeée de sa misère*, detested *les plaisirs*, liked only her regular everyday work and *la paix*.

'Here we have a very fair *appartement*, and plenty of sunlight *au premier*. Before dinner we walked up to the Arc de 1'Etoile and back again, enjoying the lovely greenth and blossoms of the horse-chestnuts, which are in their first glory, innocent of dust or of one withered petal. This morning at twelve o'clock we are going to the Russian Church, where J. has never been, and where I hope we shall hear the wonderful intoning and singing as I heard it years ago.

'This is the chronicle of our happy married life, three days long — all its happiness conscious of a dear background in those who are loving us at Weybridge, at Thornhill, and at Ranby.

'You are all inwoven into the pattern of my thoughts, which would have a sad lack without you. I like to go over again in imagination all the scene in the church and in the vestry, and to feel every loving look from the eyes of those who were rejoicing for us. Write us word about everything and consider yourselves all very much loved and spiritually petted by your loving sister.'

Charles was not forgotten; he was sent an account of the view from Grenoble and the Grande Chartreuse. 'I had but one regret in seeing the sublime beauty of the Grande Chartreuse. It was that Pater had not seen it. I would still give my life up willingly if he could have the happiness instead of me. But marriage seems to have restored me to my old self. I was getting hard, and if I had decided differently, I think I should have become very selfish. To feel daily the loveliness of a nature close to me, and to feel grateful for it, is the fountain of tenderness and strength to endure.'

Here I put down the book and stared into the gas fire, trying to reconcile two pictures: the bridegroom whose loveliness of nature gave her strength to endure and the old gentleman, short of breath, on the club sofa.

No word of illness. 'Glorious weather always, and I am very well — quite amazingly able to go through fatigue.'

Florence Cross was told that her sister-in-law was 'uninterruptedly well'. By this time the newly-weds were at Milan, where they looked forward to a 'more stationary life'. George Eliot had taken over the whole family. 'You are our children, you know,' she told Florence Cross, considerably the youngest. George Eliot's brother Isaac was thanked effusively for dropping a line. From which, I gathered, there must have been previous estrangement — over the Lewes alliance, presumably. 'The only point to be regretted in our marriage is that I am much older than he, but his affection had made him choose this lot of caring for me rather than any other of the various lots open to him.'

They were going to remain abroad, Isaac was told, until July when they would return to The Heights, Witley, Surrey.

Madame Bodichon had a long letter from Verona and Charles was the first to hear they had arrived at Venice, 'this glorious city'. But she is disappointed by the people, where every prospect pleases, they look vile. Their singing is disgraceful. 'Coarse voices much out of tune make one shudder when they strike suddenly under the window.'

But their days are passed deliciously, they see a few beautiful pictures, not hurrying too much, they have their own gondola, they 'edify' themselves with what Ruskin has written about

Venice. To top it all, they are now nearly at the end of Alfieri's autobiography which they were reading in Italian for Johnnie's better education.

Mrs Congreve, on whom Charles the dogsbody had called, had apparently written; George Eliot's next letter is to her, apologizing for the delay in replying. There is nothing to indicate in any of the letters whether Cross had edited them or not. I suspected that he had. There is a slight shuffling in this one; it is not quite truthful on the matter of dates, and hurry would not explain the tactic of sending Charles to face the music. (In future 'sending Charles' would be my way of saying 'passing the buck'.)

'I wonder whether you have imagined — I believe that you are quick to imagine for the benefit of others — all the reasons why it was left at last to Charles to tell you of the great, once-undreamed-of change in my life. The momentous decision, in fact, was not made till scarcely more than a fortnight before my marriage; and even if opportunity had left itself to my confiding everything to you, I think I could hardly have done it at a time when your presence filled me rather with a sense of your family and Emily's trouble rather than with my own affairs. Perhaps Charles will have told you that the marriage deprives no one of any good I felt bound to render before — it only gives me a more strenuous position, in which I cannot sink into the self-absorption and laziness I was in danger of before. The whole history is something like a miracle-legend. But instead of any former affection being displaced in my mind, I seem to have recovered the loving sympathy that I was in danger of losing. I mean that I had been conscious of a certain drying-up of tenderness in me, and that now the spring seems to have risen again. Who could take your place within me or make me amends for the loss of you? And yet I should not take it bitterly if you felt some alienation from me. Such alienation is very natural when a friend does not fulfil expectations of very long standing.'

The tone was curiously apologetic; if it had been addressed to a man one might surmise that his hopes had been raised. Was She apologizing for having got married or for not telling? In either case it was peculiar between one woman and another. The index showed that Mrs Congreve had a husband. Neither was connected with Lewes. What was George Eliot being so shame-faced about? Was there a lesbian element in her life? Was this what the old man wanted to tell me about? But why? Having written the most reticent biography conceivable himself, why would he want to spill the beans to a stranger? I had been sleeping very badly of late. Did I dream up that conversation on the sofa? Insomnia plays these tricks. So worried did I become that I rang up the Devonshire Club and asked the porter if Mr J.W. Cross was a member. I felt a fool as I asked the question.

'Mr Cross? He is indeed. He is a foundation member, the only one still alive.'

'I should have known that. I am very sorry for troubling you.'

'You are very welcome. 1874 — it's a long time ago, sir.'

I went back to my homework. This was the story of Rip Van Winkle. While the sixty-year-old bride was making excuses to her lady friends Johnnie did one of his disappearing tricks, and it was a surprise when he surfaced at this point.

'We thought too little of the heat, and rather laughed at English people's dread of the sun. But the mode of life at Venice had its peculiar dangers. It is one thing to enjoy heat when leading an active life, getting plenty of excercise in riding or rowing in the evenings; it is another thing to spend all one's days in a gondola — a delicious, dreamy existence — going from one church to another — from palaces to picture-galleries — sight-seeing of the most exhaustively interesting kind — traversing constantly the *piccoli rei*, which are nothing more than drains, and with bedroom-windows always open on the great drain of the Grand Canal. The effect of this continual bad air, and the complete and sudden deprivation of all bodily exercise, made me thoroughly ill. As soon as I could be moved we left Venice, on the 23rd of June, and went to Innsbruck, where we stayed for a week, and in the change to pure sweet mountain air I soon regained strength.'

After this the letters describe the slow progress home: Innsbruck, Wildbad — from where Charles hears that 'Your *Mutter* is marvellously well and strong'. Johnnie was 'inclined to linger a little in the sweet air of the Schwarzwald', Charles hears later in July. On the 22nd they are safely installed at Witley. Madame Bodichon is first to be told, with an account for her benefit of the Venice disaster.

'Mr Cross had a sharp but brief attack at Venice, due to the unsanitary influences of that wondrous city, in the later weeks of June. We stayed a little too long there, with a continuous sirocco blowing, and bad smells under the windows of the hotel; and these conditions found him a little below par from long protracted anxiety before our marriage. But ever since we left Venice (on the 23rd of June) he has been getting strong again, and we have enjoyed a leisurely journey through Germany in constant warmth and sunshine, save for an occasional thunderstorm.'

Cross was writing George Eliot's *Life*, not his own, that could explain why we never learnt until then about his being 'a little below par before our marriage'. *Long protracted anxiety*. This is the first time we had heard about it. How was it to be reconciled with the paragraph in which Johnnie told his readers about squiring George Eliot to concerts etc? Then he gave the impression of a man with no calls on his time. If he was biting his lips over neglected business at those entertainments, that was not the impression he had been at pains to create; nor was anxiety in evidence after they left Venice (with Willie who had come out to help) and travelled slowly home, nor did it prevent them from making a tour round his married sisters' establishments soon after they arrived in England.

George Eliot was assiduous about digging herself into the Cross family. This was not what interested me particularly. My eye had caught the first reference since the wedding to a return of her usual ill-health. 'I am pretty well, but find myself more languid than I was when abroad. I think the cause is perhaps the moisture of the climate. There is something languorous in this climate, or rather in its effects. J. gets a little better every day, and so each day is more enjoyable.'

I was coming very near to the end of volume three, and my finger was under the last page. Mrs Burne-Jones and Madame

Bodichon were being told about the round of visits. Charles is the first to hear of 'an attack of a mild sort', then Johnnie takes over. His intrusion has the air of an obituary, so much so that I peeped ahead to see if her letters began again. There were a few. Before we are allowed to read them Cross tells us that there had been a recurrence of the renal disorder of the previous year. Ten days in Brighton for a 'bracing change' failed to do the trick. Dr Andrew Clark, 'the beloved physician', came down to consult with Mr Parsons of Godalming. There was a 'gradual but slow improvement' and during November, a decided recovery of strength . . .

'I had never seen my wife out of England, previous to our marriage, except the first time at Rome, when she was suffering. My general impression, therefore, had been that her health was always very low, and that she was almost constantly ailing. Moreover, I had been with her very frequently during her long severe illness at Witley in 1879. I was the more surprised, after our marriage, to find that from the day she set foot on Continental soil, till the day she returned to Witley, she was never ill — never even unwell. She began at once to look many years younger. During the eleven years of our acquaintance I had never seen her so strong in health. The greater dryness and lightness of the atmosphere seemed to have a magical effect. At Paris we spent our mornings at the Louvre or the Luxembourg, looking at pictures or sculpture, or seeing other sights — always fatiguing work. In the afternoons we took long walks in the Bois, and very often went to the theatre in the evening. Reading and writing filled in all the interstices of time: yet there was no consciousness of fatigue . . . Decrease of physical strength coincided exactly with the time of our return to the damper climate of England . . . Towards the middle of October she was obliged to keep her bed, but without restriction as to amount of reading and talking, which she was always able to enjoy, except in moments of acute pain.'

On December 3rd they moved to 4 Cheyne Walk. Next day they were at a concert. Dr and Mrs Congreve called, so did Madame Belloc. The readings aloud were in full spate (Max Muller's *Lectures on the Science of Language*, Duffield's translation *of Don Quixote, Hermann and Dorothea*, Tennyson's latest poems, and Mr Myer's volume on Wordsworth). They were having no end of fun. On Friday December 17th, the insatiable couple went to see *Agamemnon* performed in Greek by Oxford undergraduates. It was not what I would have prescribed for a delicate woman who had not been well, but it proved 'a great enjoyment — an exciting stimulus'. So much so that She proposed the Greek tragedies for reading aloud that winter. She must have quite recovered because next day they went to another concert. 'It was a cold day. The air in the hall was over-heated, and George Eliot allowed a fur cloak which she wore to slip from her shoulders. I was conscious of a draught . . .'

That evening She played some of the pieces they had been listening to at the concert 'with a touch as true and as delicate as ever'. On Sunday there was 'very slight trouble in the throat', but She felt well enough to see visitors. After they left She began a letter to Mrs Strachey. It broke off after a few sentences. On Monday the doctor treated her for a 'laryngeal sore throat'. Dr Andrew Clark came for consultation on Wednesday evening. Then Cross: 'Whilst the doctors were at her bedside, she had just time to whisper to me, "Tell them I have great pain in the left side." ' They were her last words.

II

Colin

HE WAS WAITING for me in the hall, fluttering about, dressed up for the occasion, resplendent in his Edwardian waistcoat; his shoes, old but hand-made, shone; he wore a silk cravat. He was staring at every face that came through the door so intently that I slipped in under his gaze and greeted him first. He started, then took in who I was and what had happened, and I thought for a moment that he was going to hug me.

'Well, this *is* delightful.'

If his voice crackled a little, it was rich and sonorous. As he stepped out, leading the way, he had the air of a man who had been athletic in his day; there was nothing epicene about him. It upset one of my theories about the unlikely marriage.

He had gone to no end of trouble, I could see, had been plotting with the waiter, knew our table, and led me to it; although I avoid substantial meals in the middle of the day when I can, I hadn't the heart to turn down all the elaborate arrangements he had made for my entertainment. We began with a champagne cocktail.

The fluttering manner was catching; both of us twittered, outdoing each other in civilities while time galloped away. Whenever we seemed to have settled down at last, he thought of something to ask the waiter; subsequent efforts to catch his attention were as slow as a game of Test cricket. When, after half an hour, his fussy concern subsided, he stared round him with complacency as God did on His creation. I thought we were ready now to come down to business, and I wanted us to start in Venice. I was at home there, and I was curious to learn more about that sudden attack of fever. There had been some covering up, but of what? I had to suppress a groan when he began: 'Well I remember the first time Henry James dined with me here.' This was what I wanted to get away from, literary gossip, the sort of thing I had spent months mugging up for that thin book of mine. He did not observe my reaction — my mouth was full when he began. I was gagged.

'We were at the table over there in the window — spring of '78, I think it was — seems like yesterday. I had Lewes to meet him, and my cousin Alex Sellar, and my brother-in-law Henry Hall (Bullock as he was then), and I can't for the life of me remember who else. Capital talk. Lewes could be most entertaining, especially when there were no women about. His discretion about what could be said before the ladies was always rather suspect. I never told him so, of course. I couldn't have, could I? It was a small fault: he had had a rather patchy start in life, one had to remember. He was at his amusing best that evening; we talked until midnight, and when we came out it was raining cats and dogs and not a hansom in sight . . .'

'You knew Henry James?' The journalist in me asked that question automatically. Had he not said so? Why was I encouraging him to waste my time?

'Pretty well, not intimately. But who knew that arcane individual intimately? He called on me at Cheyne Walk when my dear one died, and was beautifully sympathetic — he had written me a pleasant letter when we got married — I really liked him that day, and I talked rather indiscreetly. No doubt you read what *he said* I said. I was upset about it at the time, but he was dead. He wouldn't have published it in my lifetime.'

I hadn't the least idea what Johnnie was talking about. I tried to look as if I did. I was still under surveillance.

'As if I would have said to Henry James (or to anyone) that if She hadn't died when She did, She would have killed me . . . H.J. was a most unreliable reporter of facts: he couldn't resist a little embroidering, if only to give a better shape to a sentence, and the dramatist in him was always on the look-out for material.'

Having said this in his usual fruity voice, my host looked cautiously round the room, then leaning across the table, in what was intended as *sotto voce* — it must have been audible in the pantry — added for my benefit, 'Though I think She would have, you know.'

Then, in his usual crackle, as if thinking aloud, 'I *do* remember saying something to the effect that we were like a cart horse yoked to a racer. But how many people could have kept up with her? Intellectually, I mean. It was very naughty of James to put my confidence down on paper. We had talked intimately as friends at a time of grief. He never let on. The last time I met him he reminded me of the conversation and solemnly asked my permission to use it (disguised, of course) as a plot for a short story — *Fever in Venice*.'

'He never did?' I interrupted anxiously.

'No. No. It was very shortly before his death, poor fellow.'

My face must have fallen: so James had been told my story; Gosse — how many others? I would have to take soundings. John Walter Cross was possibly famous for this ploy, his way of making himself interesting. Our fellow members may have been laughing among themselves at the Ancient Mariner's most recent victim. It was a pity he got on to Henry James in the first place, and most difficult to prise him off, but I did it at last when I was given a solemn assurance that James had never heard the *whole* story. The wariness that had crept into my manner must have come through to him; he became suddenly solicitous about my entertainment.

'Is the Sauternes to your liking? I took the liberty of ordering it without waiting to take you into consultation. I last drank it here with Turgenev, about twenty years before you were born I'd say. There was one bottle left, and I thought the coincidence too remarkable to let slip. A good omen, don't you agree? Your health, Colin: and will you please call me "Johnnie". I like to think of you in the magic circle.'

I had thrown my hand in by this time, and I can't remember what we talked about. Anything was as likely as not to spark off an anecdote or call up a name. He had met everyone in his time, it seemed, and as we travelled round and round our subject without ever coming to land my misgivings were confirmed, the story was a ruse to capture an audience. The old man was lonely, he wanted to reminisce to somebody who would recognize his allusions.

'I don't know where to begin,' he said. The hands of the dining-room clock stood at half past three. We had been sitting there for two hours and a half. My face must have reflected an inward grimace. He had been truly hospitable, but I had been lured to lunch on false pretences. I looked at my watch and said I had to go.

'But we haven't even begun. We must repeat this pleasant occasion in the very near future. I would like very much to entertain you at Chester Square. Mrs Patterson, my housekeeper — I abducted her from Sevenoaks when my sister died — I'm sure Mrs Patterson would like nothing better than an excuse to make her *crème caramel*. She is very proud of it. Some Sunday, perhaps. Are you free at week-ends as a rule?'

'I am usually in Scotland, if I can manage it. My fiancée lives in Edinburgh.'

'Ah, yes. Of course . . .'

Before he had another brainwave I thought the time had come when I must show that I couldn't be played with like this. The initiative had been taken by him. After two conversations I was no wiser about what he had in mind. If I stood my ground he must deliver. It was not as if I came unarmed. I had questions to ask. The afternoon lay in ruins all about us in any case. I might as well throw in the little that was left.

'Could we sit somewhere else? I am sure the staff is longing to get us out of the dining-room.'

His face lit up; he had been resigning himself to my departure.

'That suits me admirably, but I feel guilty about the inroads I am making on the valuable time of a very busy man. Would you like a cigar?'

'No, thank you.'

I let him lead the way to the sofa on which our strange acquaintance had begun. There was sun in this room; except for a few rather sad-looking lone figures, we had the place to ourselves. I could see from his gait that my old friend was considerably braced by his good fortune, but I was determined to take control of what was left of the day. It took him by surprise when I ignored his first fatuous observation and said that I had been reading his biography 'again' (I lied).

'Oh, yes.'

He looked rather shifty then, not liking the idea of my running loose.

'I had a lot of trouble with that book. I felt that I had to write it. God knows what might have happened if some of her friends had taken it on themselves. She was enormously concerned about her "influence". She had very high views about a writer's responsibility to the public, and especially one like herself to whom many, very many people looked for a moral lead. She was much afraid that her marriage would undermine her "influence". That explains why she was so shy about telling her friends she was marrying me. The idea that she might be getting any pleasure out of it was the trouble. After her extremes of grief when Lewes died, which were well-known, she was in a quandary. She satisfied her own conscience by the observation that she had begun to hug her grief and become selfish, but that was not a thought she could communicate to the world. It fitted in with one of her favourite lines in Dante. Do you know Italian?'

'Not really.'

' "There is not virtue in gloom, which is the easiest hiding-place for languid idleness." That is a very loose translation, but it makes the point.'

'There is one question I have wanted to ask you, but somehow we never got round to it. May I ask it now?'

Again that child-caught-in-the-pantry look.

'If I can answer it?'

'What happened in Venice?'

'In *Venice*?'

He looked very shifty now.

'You went to Venice with George Eliot in June 1880 — the year my mother was born, incidentally. Suddenly you became extremely ill. There was no hint of it in the letters you quote from. What happened exactly?'

'I thought I had made that quite clear. A nasty drain under our window, heat, no exercise, noxious smells. You know Venice. I don't have to tell *you*.'

'Why didn't you change your hotel?'

'That is being wise after the event.'

'On the 10th of June you had been already in Venice for ten days and were hoping to stay on for as much longer. There is not a word in the letters about noxious smells.'

'Not in the letters, I grant you, but it is hardly a subject one would raise in a letter. I inserted a paragraph in the biography. There was no mystery about it.'

'Your wife was in splendid health throughout the honeymoon?'

'Could we use another word? *Honeymoon* has a rather cheap sound to my ear. "Wedding Journey" was what it used to be called. In answer to your question: Yes. She was.'

'Better than she had been for years?'

'That is true. She was up with the lark. Nothing would prevent her from starting out before the city was awake. Our gondolier hadn't come on duty yet, but She didn't object to walking about when the city was empty of tourists. I was in a trance most of the time, not having had my quota of sleep, and feeling distinctly under par in any case. But the early morning air and the breeze that came from the sea across the lagoon was refreshing. Venice is at its best very early. Later in the day, when the sun was at its height, the stench from the canal under our hotel was distinctly unpleasant at times.

'That was the pattern of our days. I had married her perfectly resigned to the prospect of having an invalid on my hands. I accepted the responsibility. Not only because I was devoted to her but from a conviction that people of genius have the right to expect that return from ordinary mortals. We are so much in their debt. But you are quite right. From the moment her foot lighted on foreign soil there was no holding her. Indefatigable, she was. And the livelier She became the sicker I grew. It would have made a story for Edgar Allan Poe.'

'And when you came home?'

'Oh, I was as right as rain before that. We came back via the German spas. I was soon as fit as a fiddle.'

'But She — George Eliot — became ill, did she not?'

'Indeed. Not long after we returned to England — almost at once in fact. The English climate didn't suit her.'

'She died very soon after you returned.'

'In a matter of months.'

'Not from the climate, surely?'

'I don't think She would have died so soon if we had lived abroad.'

'Did you ever suggest it?'

'We talked about it. She was enthusiastic at the idea of a new life, but that was euphoric. She was excited by our journey. Her enthusiasm petered out. We began the adventure too late.'

'Did She lose heart after Venice?'

Johnnie took time to answer. I saw him looking at me from the back of his eyes.

'What made you say that?'

'You got ill in Venice, didn't you?'

'Who told you that?'

'It's in your book.'

'It may have discouraged her certainly.'

We looked at each other like boxers in the ring. He was holding something back. I knew it. He knew I knew it. But what could I say? He had waylaid me to give me the subject for a book. This should have been the moment of truth. Defeated, I rose to go. He lacked the nerve to detain me, and there was something almost abject in his manner as he saw me to the door.

'Thank you for an excellent lunch.' That it had been. But I had been sold short. To do him credit he did not say anything about a meeting in the future. I looked back as I turned into Piccadilly. He was standing where I left him, looking after me.

The trouble was that I couldn't hope to avoid him unless I gave up using my club, and I didn't want to do that. I was beginning to feel at home there. I had been gratified when my former chief had proposed me for membership. It suited me in every way. A greater man might have ignored the nuisance, but I am a moral coward, desperately easy to blackmail because I have never been able to shake off a vague sense of guilt towards the world in general. What it is about I have yet to discover, an inborn feeling of unworthiness, I suppose. In any event, whatever the reason for my diffidence, it threatened to wreck my life as a clubman. But I made myself go. I met the sad glance, like a lover's who has gone too far too fast, and is at a loss how to return to the jumping-off place. And, of course, I felt sorry for his loneliness, although it was no business of mine. Sometimes he greeted me cheerfully, sometimes wistfully. We had a dog at home when I was a child who behaved in exactly the same way. In the end I would capitulate. If only because I was still curious to discover whether there was something more and, I told myself, when my grandchildren hear that I knew George Eliot's husband they may well take me to task for not pursuing the acquaintance.

I suppose part of the trouble was my lack of enthusiasm for the lady herself. She was too solemn for me. Anyhow, I ignored his longing looks; and then one day I came into the dining-room and there he was fussing over a guest as he had fussed over me. I looked to see who it was and felt outraged when I recognized Malcolm Gladd. Gladd is one of the lowest forms of life, one of the new-fangled gossip-column journalists, none of whom is allowed into decent clubs. The old man must have become lost to any sense of shame if he was reduced to such company. It was hardly my place as a new member to report him, but I was sure if the committee knew what was happening, someone would be delegated the unpleasant duty of whispering in Cross's better ear that his guest was *persona non grata* with the members.

It was the measure of his loneliness, I supposed, but the journalist in me was piqued to see what I had brought about by my intolerance and impatience. Gladd would have none of my diffidence. He would extract every morsel of juicy meat there was in the Cross cupboard, and skeletons, if any.

The fellow is incorrigible. He caught my eye and had the confounded cheek to raise his glass, thereby drawing me in to the calamity of his presence. Cross was talking away, nineteen to the dozen; Gladd, no doubt, was hearing all about Venice, and the conversation would be relayed on Sunday to readers of his loathsome column. I cursed myself. They left the dining-room before I did; I visualized them spread out over *our* sofa while the silly old man gave his all; but I was wrong. Gladd was waiting for a taxi when I came out, and he greeted me like an old friend, ignoring my distinctly chilly nod. I suppose a hide of reinforced concrete is a *sine qua non* with these pests.

'I was lunching with George Eliot's relict. Quaint old bird. I didn't know you were a member there. Since when? He is quite incontinent, rambling on, said he had a wonderful story to tell me, and I was quite prepared to listen; in my line of business it's all grist to the mill. But all I got was an affidavit about the spotlessness of his virgin youth. I couldn't see what business that was of mine, and I only hope he wasn't the cause of too much disappointment to the ladies of his acquaintance. But someone ought to keep an eye on him. Next thing we shall be hearing is some unfortunate incident in the park. There's a taxi.Can I drop you anywhere?'

I refused the offer, but I was well content. Gladd was too pig-ignorant to realize the possibilities of the Cross-Eliot story. Luckily for me. And my old friend would have put him off by mentioning all the people he had told it to. Gladd didn't want an *old* story. Something would go into his newspaper, but not what I had been promised. If Cross had a secret I was going to worm it out of him. I didn't care how long it took me. The Ancient Mariner was a nuisance in his time, but what a good story Coleridge got out of *him*.

But I couldn't refrain from teasing Johnnie when I joined him at the bar next time I was in the club. I was mean enough to hint that his unsuitable guest had prattled to me.

'It's their own fault if people refuse to talk to them or let them into clubs. They are abusing their privileges. Where did you come across Gladd? I wouldn't have thought you would have had any time for him.'

'I have loads of time. It's the only thing I have on my hands these days. I didn't tell him anything that mattered. I have been reproaching myself since our last luncheon. I have taken advantage of your kind interest. But you see, if I don't fill the background in, how are you to appraise the situation? I must make sure you get the story right. I left so much out of that book of mine. At the time I thought I was doing the loyal thing, but I greatly fear the result has been to make George Eliot seem a bore. Young people have said as much. And She wasn't you know. She was *tremendous*.'

'Could we lunch here on Friday?'

An impulse, a generous impulse, I would like to think; he almost exploded with pleasure.

I was sorry when the time came that I had not chosen a new pitch, if only because I had the distinct impression that we were a source of amusement to the older members — very much more in evidence than my own contemporaries — and it would have been better strategy from my point of view. However, apart from his over-eagerness when I arrived — he was half afraid that I would let him down — he seemed more assured to-day. I felt there was something in the air, a nice surprise for me. For once he made no fuss over the preliminaries. I was in charge, of course, but even so he had a spoilt baby's genius for complicating the simplest routine. We had finished the unsympathetic melon that was lunch's overture when he felt in his pocket and took out an envelope; this he handed to me.

'What is it?'

'See for yourself.'

We must have looked like a chorus girl and her protector in a successful gold-digging operation.

A very old letter with Queen Victoria on the stamp, addressed to J.W. Cross Esq., City Liberal Club, Walbrook, London EC. I looked at the date — 16 October 1879. Lewes was not yet a year dead. The Cross wedding was six months away.

In deference to his excitement, I held the envelope as if it were made of the finest glass and waited for him to tell me to open it. He seemed to like this. His face was creased with encouraging smiles.

'Go on, you may read it. I'll show you everything. But this *is* rather special, I'll admit.'

I was, of course, intensely curious, but something more and nobler was expected of me. Could I supply it?

'Best loved and loving one', it began. Suddenly embarrassed, as if he was exposing himself, I looked across the table to see if he was thinking better of his action. His eyes were fixed on me. He was waiting eagerly, and gave me an impatient nod to get on with it. I hurried then, afraid he might have a stroke.

She wrote of his 'eyes of love' and went on at once into self-pity about her pain, the world's suffering, her own chill and headache. She praised his goodness. What did it matter that he knew nothing of Hiphil or Hophal or metaphysics or the works of Kepler in science. He knew the better things that belonged to the manly heart, lovingness and rectitude. Then she turned to business, something about a legal document. Love forgotten, she went on to discuss an article in the *New Quarterly*. Then a final paragraph of tenderness. She was thinking of him playing tennis, waiting for a letter from him, more anxious for his life than her own. She closed with Virgil's stricture on woman's mutability, but signed herself his 'tender Beatrice'.

I didn't look up at once, not knowing quite what was expected of me. The whole had been such an odd mixture of self-pity, affection, condescension, and bathos — a letter to a child. I pretended to read it through again. I was playing for time. There was some disappointment in his voice when he said, 'That was her first love letter to me. I thought you might like to see it. I never expected to show it to a soul.'

'You must treasure it. Thank you very much for the compliment you have paid me.'

'I trust you, Colin.'

'It would make a splendid beginning to the story.'

'What story?'

'The one you said you were going to tell me.'

'Oh, *that.*'

'I am longing to hear it. What James and Gosse never heard and would have given their ears for.'

I thought I caught a slightly guilty expression on his baby face.

'Forgive me. I have been unconscionably slow about getting down to business. You must take a share of the blame, young man. I enjoy these meetings so much that I am afraid I am inclined to forget that your time is far too valuable to be wasted on an old buffer's reminiscences. Once I get started I can't stop. I get carried away. Mrs P. is always warning me against it. I don't always heed her good advice. I do so love a chat.'

'So do I, but I feel that we have rather taken our time about formulating a plan for this book. I still haven't the faintest idea what you have in mind.'

'I'm glad you said that; the truth is, I have been having misgivings about the whole enterprise.'

'About your choice of a collaborator, you mean?'

'Heavens! No. You have no idea — you would be flattered if you knew how often I congratulate myself about acting on that hunch. It took me all my courage at the time to introduce myself to you like that. I did it on brandy. Our talks have given me a new interest in life, and when you get to my age you won't need to be told what a miracle that is. The trouble is, you have stirred up so much that was peacefully asleep. You have made me look at a great many things I had left behind me with new eyes. It is a disturbing experience, makes one doubt the truth of everything, even one's own motives. At the time one didn't question them. I am rewriting a great deal of my own history. It makes me appreciate Jesting Pilate's question, what is truth? Sometimes, it seems to me, the answer depends upon the state of one's digestion.'

'Here we go,' I said to myself. I must pull in the line. What a dab he was at getting off the hook of a question.

'You were saying that you had misgivings.'

'Indeed. One voice tells me that I am a very lucky man to have come across anyone so sympathetic and intelligent as yourself, whom I can trust to report me aright. A more cautious small voice advises me to let sleeping dogs lie. At the time all I could think of was raising monuments and looking after my Beatrice's reputation. When She died I was bereft. Talk about Othello, I had allowed her concerns to occupy my whole existence. I could still look after her reputation. That occurred to me when I made the decision to write her life. She was enormously preoccupied with her reputation — as a woman, not as a novelist, you understand. I believe that She was well aware of her literary worth. The other was what required careful handling. She did not ask me to do it — frankly, I think She would have preferred someone of greater eminence. She might have thought of Lord Acton, a fervent admirer, or Jowett. But none of these came forward, and I didn't want to hand her over to one of the worshipping women. God alone knows what havoc one of them might have created. Better not to dwell on it.

'In the circumstances, I felt sure that I was doing what She would have approved. We talked about the subject quite a lot during the last few weeks. She must have had a premonition that the end was in sight. She had considered an autobiography in the past but rejected the idea on two grounds: a writer of fiction puts as much of himself as he requires — sometimes more than he realizes — into his stories. What he keeps back may be known to his doctor or lawyer, his family even; but it is what he was not willing to share with the world. His wishes must be respected by biographers. Her principal objection to autobiographies was the dragging of other people in as supporting characters in the writer's own story.'

'I can't follow you.'

'The autobiographer must necessarily bring his friends and acquaintances into his account of his life, and not as they might always choose to appear. George Eliot saw this as taking liberties, invading their privacy. She was morbidly scrupulous.'

'But I should have thought there was far more grief among the people left out than was felt by anyone brought in. Here was a chance of vicarious immortality. I don't think much of that argument.'

'Take the case of Herbert Spencer.'

'What about him?' I asked. Johnnie was for ever making surprise attacks on my limited supply of bookish knowledge.

'He, as you probably know, was very close to George Eliot for a few years; they remained lifelong friends.'

I did remember his name cropping up in the three-volume *Life*. It seemed eminently skippable at the time.

'Spencer was a philosopher of a sort?' I ventured.

'Is that his epitaph or a question? In either case my answer would be "yes".'

I don't think Johnnie intended to put me down. He was too engrossed in his subject.

'George Eliot met him at the time She was helping Chapman on the *Westminster Review*. Spencer was greatly impressed by her, he said no one else combined intellect with imagination to the extent that She did. She was one of the few people that he deigned to talk to. He was bloody rude to most people. He talked to her a lot; they were to be seen out walking, not only in London, talking their heads off. The rumour got about that Spencer had proposed and been refused. Neither of them, I might say, was a conventional figure of romance to look at. In Spencer's case this was not less true of his interior. When I was writing the *Life* I hinted delicately at *tendresse*. I thought Spencer (who lived to a great age and never married) would be flattered to go down in history holding George Eliot's hand — if only for a moment — but I was wrong. Spencer took my reference in bad part, when I sent it to him for his approval (I was over-conscientious in this respect) and when I re-drafted it he still objected. He wanted me to deny the rumour flatly. I was not going to say that there was nothing between them. She had told me otherwise, and I wanted to put someone distinguished among her beaux. When the *Life* came out he was very cross, and in his temper — which he regretted later — he told me that so far from his having proposed to her and been refused, She had proposed to him, and he had turned down the offer. He had a letter to prove it. His vanity was hurt by the suggestion that he could want to marry anyone so plain to look at. How caddish of him. These so-called great men! Pah.'

'There are no Spencers alive now. You can say what you please. No one can stop you.'

'I know. You don't have to tell *me*, but you must sympathize with my predicament. I went to such lengths to cover her tracks. I even falsified evidence. The habit so grew on me that I could leave nothing alone; I changed "legs" to "arms" in the interests of decency.'

'Anyone who required that protection should have seen a doctor.'

'I was the dotty one, not She. I shouldn't have taken the task on. Wasn't up to it. I was diffident from the start, but when I consulted Acton he said that one couldn't go wrong if She was let speak for herself from letters and diaries. I never confessed to him that I was not only editing the material, but cutting out anything that I thought might throw doubts on the truth of my portrait of her.'

'Are your misgivings, then, about the past? That would be a waste of time. What you must concentrate on now is the new book. What shape is it to have? Could we consider that before we get lost again in all this fascinating detail?'

'Let me put my dilemma in a nutshell. One side of me lives in dread of this Strachey fellow — look what he did to Florence Nightingale. I hate to think what he would do to my loved one if he knew half of what I know; and I would cut a sorry figure in the process. Not that I care about that for myself, but the nieces . . . You know how it is . . . What keeps me awake at night is the thought that it will be the excessive care I bestowed on her reputation that will leave her open to cruel jibes. Should I then, with your help, put the record straight while I can? Or is that a signal to the debunkers that more evidence for the prosecution may be available? I should say "persecution", because that is what it has become. I am in a fix. No-one can help me.'

'Let me try.'

'My dear Colin. What a good fellow you are. Do you not think that the wisest course in the end might be to let her books do the job? There they are on the shelf, imperishable, but somewhat neglected at the moment. Never mind, I say, their turn will come. All this talk about Hardy — Hardy isn't a patch on her.'

'You could make her seem more human. It is her air of propriety that puts off the present generation. She is so earnest.'

'But She wasn't you know — not all the time. She liked a laugh as much as anyone when She felt sure of her company. Perhaps I should leave it there and trust to time.'

'Then, are you prepared to run the risk of Strachey or some other debunker doing his worst?'

'Damn Strachey. What times we live in. No-one is safe; nothing is sacred. But if in the effort to avert an imaginary threat we do the damage ourselves, I am going to look a fool.'

'Is there a great deal of material then that you thought unpublishable when you were writing the *Life*?'

I was being disingenuous. He was too decent to suspect it.

'I left out a lot, the picture-restorer who wanted to marry her — the only proposal of marriage She ever had —'

'But surely —'

'I never *proposed* in so many words. I don't wonder you look surprised, but I have been raking over the past with extraordinary thoroughness these nights (and days, indeed) and I have no recollection of ever popping the question. When She said I had done it three times, I was surprised, but I never contradicted her.'

'What happened to the picture-restorer?'

'Nothing.'

'Poor chap.'

'But, did he propose? We don't know. We don't even know his name. He asked permission indirectly to pay his addresses. Nothing came of it.'

'I thought that She was a scrupulously honest person.'

'Certainly, but in emotional matters, her imagination played a significant part; and, then, She was given to hysteria. What people don't realize —'

Here he stopped to make sure no-one was listening, then boomed so that anyone who cared to listen would not have missed a word,

'What no-one realizes is that she was a woman of strong passions.'

Having said this, he became abstracted. I had grown accustomed to the way he had of turning stones over in the road and then forgetting I was there while he examined what he found underneath. When he started to talk again it was more to himself than to me.

'I had no idea, none. I didn't think decent women had, not in the circle I moved in. And not at sixty, in any event. At forty I knew nothing about women, absolutely nothing.'

'What I find difficult to understand is why you waited until after you were married to face the problem. Surely you could have —'

'But I did, young sir.'

'Did what?'

'The awful possibility struck me as soon as I spoke to Charles. She couldn't face it — telling him that She was going to marry me. She implored me to do it for her. I didn't fancy the task, not in the least. Would *you* have? Asking a man nearly as old as myself if he had any objection to my marrying his mother? She wasn't, of course, nor his stepmother either if we are going by the book. It was like another scene for *Hamlet*.'

He paused there, to contemplate it, I suppose; then, as if seeking help,

'It is so difficult to talk of such things.'

'Of course.'

'But what a relief to meet someone who speaks one's own language. Between ourselves, Mrs P. takes every opportunity she can to bring up the subject by hinting at difficulties with the late Mr P. who, I gather, was mildly addicted to draught beer and considerably older than Mrs P. "I don't know how it might have been if the positions had been reversed", she says and waits for a titbit from me. I am not reduced to that. Not yet, and, please God, never shall be. I have reason to be grateful that the women I have known were noble characters. But I must acknowledge that Mrs P. does her best to make me comfortable.'

'What did Charles say?'

'Oh, there was no trouble with *him*. He met me on the threshold, so to speak. I hadn't even to complete my opening sentence; he was all good will. He said he was grateful for my attentions to George Eliot, assured me that he had no misgivings. His father would have been comforted had he known that I would take his place; she needed so much looking-after. As for himself, he had long regarded me as his brother. I said his mother — or "mutter" as he called her, German, you know, because, of course, she wasn't his mother — was afraid that he might see it as infidelity to his father's memory. He said that was to forget how unjealous and open-hearted his father was, the last to grudge her any chance of happiness. Of course — and I was not unmindful of it at the time — I was taking some of the pressure off Charles. She did make a lot of use of him, and he had his own wife and family to look after as well as his job and intellectual hobbies. He had unrealized aspirations like so many sons of famous fathers.

'I hadn't relished the assignment, and I went back to the Priory to report, feeling enormously relieved. I found her surrounded by women with pins in their mouths and cloths of every colour in the spectrum laid out on chairs and a general impression of new ribbons and old lace running wild. An Aladdin's Cave effect, but the cause of it all looked weirdly out of place in her black gown and shawl, a character from another play. It was certainly no place for me. When I came in She was trying on a bonnet. I saw her looking wistfully at the effect in the glass of the straw butterfly perched on that massive head. She saw me then; her eyes asked the question. I gave her the thumbs-up sign.

'The watchful Brett, her maid, took charge of me then. I was led into the study where *The Times* was laid out and offered tea or whatever refreshment I required at half-past three in the afternoon. I could only think of lemonade. (Brett, needless to say, was in the secret.) I was reading about the clean sweep the Liberals had made at the elections when my dear one came in at last, her colour up, all apologies and confusion. I caught a glimpse in that moment of Mary Anne Evans; and then George Eliot, every line of whose face was so familiar, came beside me and began at once,

' "What did he say?"

' "He seemed delighted, couldn't have been more reassuring, said it was what his father would have wished."

' "Start at the beginning. I want to hear every word."

'I knew this was true. George Eliot was a wonderful listener. Novelists tend to be, I suspect. You are, Colin, bless you. I told her everything as I remembered it, but I had to edit myself as I went along. I didn't tell her, for instance, that Charles said she would be getting solid comfort from being *Mrs* Somebody at last. She had suffered more than anyone imagined from having to live without the legal status of a married woman. It seemed to her so unfair that lifelong total commitment such as existed between her and his father was given a dishonourable name when people who had nothing in common and were unfaithful to each other were called man and wife. And, of course, I didn't tell her that he said I was being noble in sacrificing the usual joys of marriage. I had to be diplomatic, you understand, and I was driven to repeating myself. She came to the rescue.

' "Dear Charles; such a good fellow. I was afraid he might be difficult. He was so devoted to his father. What you say about his twice having welcomed you as a brother interests me particularly." (He had only said it once; it was I who had said it twice. I let it be. I was grateful, I must admit. It was generous of him.)

' "What surprises me is that if he felt like that about you it didn't put him off the whole plan," she said after an awkward pause.

' "I don't follow. He seemed to be welcoming me into the family or, perhaps I should say, treating me as if I were already a member of it."

' "Exactly; did it not surprise you?"

' "His cordiality? It flattered me certainly, and I was relieved to notice no sign of resentment. He might well have said I was a poor substitute for his father."

'Here she gave me a look which always made me feel uncomfortable, as if I were something on a plate.

' "The gods were generous with their gifts to you. You should take pride in them."

'She must have known by now that I did not know how to respond to that sort of compliment. The jolly atmosphere at home had not prepared me for it. But she didn't wait for my reaction. She was on a trail. She would not be put off it.

' "If he regards you as his brother, he must be deeply shocked by our plan."

' "It was a figure of speech."

' "Figures of speech have more significance than scientific classifications. This is like a Greek tragedy. I hope he won't come to see it that way when he broods over the matter."

' "I don't think he is going to brood. He seems thoroughly pleased with the arrangement," I assured her.

' "Ah, maybe. But you said that he twice referred to you as his brother."

' "I may have exaggerated. Perhaps he only said it once. On reflection, I think he *did* only say it once."

' "But the fact that *you* made that mistake shows how great an impression he must have made on you."

' "I was grateful. It was the warmest and kindest thing he could have said in the circumstances. I shouldn't attach too much significance to it."

' "I don't, but I think you must now see why I let you break the news to him. You are the nearest thing on earth to man before the Fall. The implications of our plan would have been too much for me. If Charles had told me that he regarded you as his brother I couldn't have gone on with it. I'd have broken down."

' "Why? I don't understand. I thought he gave exactly the sort of reassurance you were looking for."

' "Johnnie, dear. Was all that money spent on sending you to Rugby entirely wasted? Does Oedipus not come to mind?"

' "Of course not."

' "I love when you put on that disapproving voice. We cannot be such hypocrites as to say we derive great advantages from reading the classics and then pretend to be shocked when we see their themes enacted in real life. That is insincere and superficial. It makes education a waste of time.''

' ''Oedipus killed his father and married his mother. With the best will in the world I can't see the slightest resemblance to my own experience.''

' ''How literal you are. Use your imagination. If you are Charles's brother and I am Charles's mother, then I must be your mother. Charles must see that if you are marrying his mother you are marrying your own mother. I would expect him to be startled by the notion of incest.''

' ''But this is all nonsense. You are not Charles's mother or even his step-mother, and I am certainly not his brother. All three of us are strangers in blood, and there is nothing in our marriage he can object to. In any case . . . ''

'I didn't want to finish that sentence, but she made me.

' ''In any case?''

' ''Oh, nothing. I had said all I wanted to say.''

' ''Not quite all. You were going to qualify it.''

' ''I was not, I assure you.''

' ''One doesn't begin a sentence with 'In any case' without having some reservation in mind. This is too important; you must be honest and say out whatever it is. That was the principle on which George and I conducted our marriage. In the end it was hardly necessary to speak. Each knew what the other was thinking.''

' ''I was going to say, but I didn't because it seemed so obvious, that our marriage was of a very different nature to Oedipus's.''

' ''He didn't have the benefit of a Church of England ceremony, as we will. Is that what you mean?''

' ''Yes'', I lied.

'I was fully aware of the implications of what she was saying, and if she had been a man would have told her plainly what I thought of the analogy, but I wasn't accustomed to having this sort of conversation with women.'

'She was before her time wasn't She? This is Freud country. He sees sex as the source of most of our behaviour.'

'So I gather, but I don't see why we should throw over morality at the bidding of a Jewish doctor.'

'The fact remains that the existence of an Oedipus complex has been generally recognized.'

'Not by me. My nieces are always talking about their "inferiority complexes". I tell them to use plain English. "Shyness" is what they mean, and a very good thing it is in young girls and wasn't invented only yesterday. It's a notion that has been around for quite a long time.'

Another distraction was raising its head. I would not allow myself to be sidetracked by Dr Freud or his disciples, and if I argued with Johnnie he would only lose his temper. I played with the crumbs on my plate and waited for him to cool down. I could not believe that George Eliot's admission of awareness of the fact of incest, at the age of sixty, could still be bothering him. We were in a sensitive area certainly, but it had nothing to do with unnatural vice.

'We are having an extraordinary conversation, you know. Do you realize that I am telling you things that I have never confided in a soul?'

'I appreciate it.' After that I didn't know how to say that we seemed to me to be marooned. He too, perhaps, was waiting for the impression left by the unhappy intrusion of Freud to fade. When he resumed the conversation I got the impression of someone who had decided to take a line. Hitherto he had been going round in circles of ever-increasing embarrassment.

'I told you She said I was like man before the Fall, and I must have been an innocent because I took it as a compliment.'

'As She meant it to be.'

'Not entirely. She was complaining about my inadequacy as a successful suitor. I refused to pick up hints, and thought at the time I was being tactful. You can see how that would exasperate a woman. When I told you just now about the way She went on about Oedipus I didn't mention its true bearing on our situation at the time. She was trying deliberately to shock me because She was exasperated by my refusal to admit to any change in our relationship. For me there hadn't been. I had only put myself in a better position to look after her, and I would be honoured to be known as George Eliot's husband. At home with my womenfolk She was like one of themselves; being married to her would be like setting up house with any of them, I thought, plus the stimulus of daily converse with such a marvellous mind. I was perfectly happy about the arrangement, the only drawback was her health, but looking after her in illness was an essential part of my devotion. I *was* devoted to her, if not quite in the way that you are devoted to your fiancée (who I am looking forward to meeting, by the way). It was another thing. I needn't labour the point. Let me say that there was an air of expectation in her manner that increasingly played on my peace of mind and made me feel ill. Everyone remarked it in my appearance. I pleaded over-work. I was in a frightful trap; marriage was only the label we put on our luggage so far as I was concerned; She saw us behaving as if we were an average young couple.'

'But you must have known cases of men marrying girls much younger than themselves; you never supposed those were father and daughter relationships, did you?'

'I kept my mind off that sort of thing.'

'But your wife-to-be was trying to make you give your mind to it for a change. Was it not to be expected? You were a fine specimen of manhood in your prime.'

'I wasn't bad-looking. Could we just leave it there?'

'She couldn't keep her . . . eyes off you, and yet you expected her to forgo her marital rights.'

'I wish you wouldn't harp on this.'

'You never supposed that She was a virgin?'

'But at her *age*.'

'You can't go by that.'

'The idea was repulsive.'

'You should have told her so before you suggested marriage.'

'It never entered my head until She brought it up, besides, as I think I told you, I have no recollection of ever having suggested marriage. It made its appearance unannounced, like mushrooms after rain.'

'I can see it was a tricky situation. You didn't want to hurt her feelings. What, in the end, did you do?'

'I had a brain wave. You remember that She consulted Sir James Paget before She accepted what She considered was my third proposal. She said it was on the question whether her marriage would undermine her "influence". What was to prevent me from consulting Sir James on my own behalf? It would be a natural precaution for a bridegroom to take. As a warm friend of hers he might well be relieved to learn for himself that She was putting herself in no danger. In the course of my visit I could let fall that She expected ours to be a complete marriage and that I had no such intention. He might be grateful for the information. She was such a delicate woman. If I could win him to my side he might, I dared to hope, even offer of his own accord to put the idea of physical intimacy out of her mind — to forbid it.

'I saw one difficulty; he might consider, even with her future husband, that he was under a professional obligation not to discuss his patient. Anticipating the difficulty, I asked our family doctor in Weybridge to refer me to him. The local worthy was embarrassed when I mentioned the subject to him and only too pleased, I could see, to hand me over to the Queen's man. I called in due course at Harewood Place and made an appointment for the following day.

'I had met the Pagets at the Pines, where they were frequent visitors, but it is another thing to meet a doctor in his consulting room. Sir James greeted me in his warm way, but I thought I saw an inquisitiveness in his glance that I had never seen there before. At this point, whenever I met him in society, he was usually petting the dog.

'He signalled to me to sit down, but remained standing himself, a procedure I found intimidating. His waiting-room was full of patients, and this was his way of saying that he had no intention of wasting time. He was a tall noble-looking creature with sad eyes. I looked for the gold watch-chain that George Eliot had given him. There it was, hanging round his neck — I had seen it before — he wore it always; today I saw it as a reminder of on whose side Sir James would be if it came to a dispute. He was quiet-voiced, gentle-mannered and, with that, somehow formidable. I could understand why, whenever there was a dispute in medical circles, he was called in to act as arbitrator, and why George Eliot had called him in to advise her about the step She was taking. For a doctor at the very top of his profession the room — obviously his study — was very plainly furnished; there was no surgical couch, or screen, or looking-glass — nothing to smooth over or delay the consultation — only straight-back chairs and a horsehair sofa of old-fashioned shape. There were portraits on the walls, all I suspected of medical heroes. Over the mantelpiece hung a young-looking oil painting of the Queen, reminding me that this man might be called at any time to inspect the Queen's naked body and, if he thought it advisable, open it with a knife. His penetrating stare made me feel uncomfortable. St. Peter might stare at one like that at the Ivory Gate: "I have summed up," those noble spaniel's eyes were saying. My uneasy glance travelled to the horsehair sofa and I imagined George Eliot stretched out on it. The thought repelled and fascinated me. How does a doctor see the human race? Does it walk about in transparencies? Is he tempted to laugh at the excessive dignity of certain venerable persons? My imagination was running amok. She had never sat in this room, much less stretched out on the couch. Sir James called on *her*, saw her in her own large bed.

' "I hear you have some condition you want to consult me about."

'I had my beginning in readiness.

' "Mrs Lewes tells me that She took you into her confidence before we decided on our wedding. Very few of her friends are in the secret."

' "She did, She did indeed. A dear and valued friend. I congratulate you, Cross. You are marrying the most distinguished woman we have in this country, or in any other, so far as I am aware."

' "She is. I know She is, but thank you. She refused to commit herself until She had consulted you."

' "Ah!"

' "Your reassurance tipped the scale. She had been extremely nervous, even as it is She has taken none of her other friends into her confidence."

' "She swore me to secrecy, but I reminded her that nothing said to her medical adviser is ever repeated."

' "As, of course, She was well aware. The precaution was unnecessary, but She may have thought that the advice She sought on this occasion not being of a medical nature, you might not have seen it as a confidence."

' "I'm sure I don't know what else you would call it. Of course, it was of a medical nature."

' "What She said to me was that She had asked you — her decision rested on your answer — whether, in your opinion, this marriage would diminish her influence."

' "Knowing how conscientious Mrs Lewes is, I would not be at all surprised if She admitted to some scruple of that description, but I must admit I can't recall her saying anything of the kind."

' "You do remember the visit?"

' "Of course; it is less than a week ago. I called on her at the Pines."

' "And She did mention that She planned to marry?"

' "That was the object of the appointment. Very properly She wanted an overhaul. We can't hide from ourselves the cruel fact that our great lady is of a certain age, but even if She were not, She was doing the right thing, in my opinion. If I had my way, I would make it compulsory for all persons before they marry to pass a rigorous medical examination. And, may I say, fit and well though you look, you show good sense by letting me run an eye over you. How long is it since you last saw a doctor?"

' "I thought my man had explained the position. My purpose in consulting you — " Here I began to feel so foolish that I was at a loss how to proceed. Sir James must have guessed my trouble.

' "Would I be right in assuming that you want to hear about your wife's fitness for marital relations? In the usual way I would advise only my patient, but as you are also my patient — I have your man's consent to this visit — I don't see why I shouldn't put your mind at ease. You are a vigorous man in the prime of life: She is much older and habitually ill. I am shocked by her drastic loss of weight since that last renal attack. The trouble is chronic — unless we decided to operate — and that I should not advise. But a great deal of her ill-health is hysterical in origin. Her nervous system is highly-tuned. In my opinion gentle conjugal intercourse might be beneficial. You would, of course, be considerate and undemanding. She was extemely solicitous on your account. It would be unfair to marry you, She said, if She were under doctor's orders to refuse her husband's reasonable expectations. Does She know you are consulting me?''

' ''No, as a matter of fact.''

' ''Pity about that. I thought She might have suggested it to put your mind at ease; women are shy about such matters. We all are. Naturally. If you take my advice you will tell her about this visit. It will greatly ease her mind. My diagnosis is that this is the best medicine we could have prescribed for her just now; She will come back from her honeymoon twenty years younger. We can expect a novel in the near future which will put everything else She has done in the shade. It will be dedicated to her husband, and he will have contributed to it in a way the world will never know.''

'The subject seemed close to Sir James's heart. He might have been leading a group of glee singers, to judge from his roseate expression. He noticed that I was in no mood to join in the chorus.

' ''I have never looked at you, don't you think I ought to since I have you here?''

' ''I am perfectly fit, thank you. I had an examination recently for an insurance policy. If I look at all strange it is because everything you have just told me takes me completely by surprise. I had no idea that Mrs Lewes expected us to have that sort of relationship. I never intended to be other than her close companion.''

' ''But, my dear sir, She will be your *wife*. Speaking as a surgeon, you understand, I should think you will find that a widow will present less embarrassment than a bridegroom usually encounters. I hear the saddest accounts of first night misadventures. I think a mother should speak very frankly to a bride-to-be. There is far too much false modesty about a perfectly natural function. If mothers won't do their duty properly, they should send their girls to see the family doctor. However, this is rather off the subject. What I intended to say: Lewes was in bad shape for the last few years — I would not be surprised — this is sheer speculation — I am betraying no confidence, mind. It may well have been some time since . . . But you will take all that into account.''

' ''Sir James,'' said I, ''would you do me a good turn? — I would be eternally in your debt — would you contrive to let Mrs Lewes know that I have no intention of making physical demands on her? I have no inclination that way. Nothing in my behaviour since we became such intimate friends could have left her under the impression. I made it clear that She was taking my mother's place.''

' ''What age are you?''

' ''Forty.''

' ''I think Mrs Lewes would laugh in my face if I gave her such a ridiculous message. May I ask you an intimate question — as between doctor and patient. Have you ever had sexual intercourse with a woman?''

' ''No.''

'The unadorned monosyllable came out at last; I had been racking my mind in vain for some suitable wrapping.

' ''Well, I can see you are shy about the whole matter, but you will find nature has a way of looking after these difficulties; she has been in the business for a long time. I often wonder about older bachelors. It is asking a lot to expect them to remain celibate all their lives, but I am sure there are a great many like yourself — God-fearing men — who manage it. Taking as much exercise as you can is a help. You are better off than the large tribe who live impeccably at home and throw the book of rules away as soon as they leave England behind them. My colleagues could tell you tales. Terrible thing to bring into a family. I shall not disgust you with the details. At least you have nothing of that sort to worry you. But if you tell your missus that you don't want to have anything to do with her conjugally you will be putting the first nail into her coffin.''

'He had a fatherly way with him, and when I left he was convinced that he had put some sense into my head. "There's a common illusion that only men like it," he said. "I don't know where that theory comes from. Nature makes the whole business plain. If you had been brought up on a farm you might smile at yourself."

'I think he believed he had convinced me. Nothing more was said. Before leaving I was taken upstairs to see the legendary wolfhound the Prince of Wales had given him. He never charged my dear one for his services, She told me, or sent a bill when Lewes died. He was very good and very grand — Sir James.

' "*She told me a lie. She told me a lie.*" I kept repeating this to myself as I walked away from Paget's house. Not indignantly, not in the least, but with a sense of relief. Dealing with George Eliot one felt oneself always at a moral disadvantage. You must have gathered this from her writings; She was longing to be treated like any other woman, but She made that difficult by being so lofty.

'When She told me I had proposed to her I didn't argue with her. I bowed and submitted to Fate. Sir James might be Surgeon-Extraordinary to the Queen, but he was not an infallible psychologist; if one thing more than another was likely to confirm my dread of the prospect before me it was that farmyard analogy. I wonder if he realized how half-hearted my handshake was at parting. But that was nothing in comparison with the fact that I had caught my beloved out in a lie. It made her so much more human. In so many matters She interpreted the signs for my benefit. I felt inadequate to argue with her and accepted her rulings from inertia. Once a fact passed through that great mind and massive imagination it became so convoluted in the process that I couldn't recognize it as the simple thing I saw before it went in.

'She had been most emphatic about the question She had put to Sir James: would her marrying injure her influence? He was eminently qualified to answer. In every sense Paget had his fingers on the pulses of the opinion-forming section of the public. Besides this, Sir James was her professed admirer. He attended Lewes in his last illness and he had been tireless in treating his son when he came back from Africa with tuberculosis of the spine. In short, a friend of the family, loved and trusted.

'None of her other friends could have kept that tit-bit of gossip to themselves. The fact remained, Sir James remembered it as a medical inquiry; the other element cannot have been stressed by her, was referred to in passing, if at all. She had been uncandid about this. George Eliot was so great that one tended to overlook in her what you would not pass in lesser folk, her skill in getting her own way, for example, by telling you what you wanted before you opened your mouth or had even given thought to the subject. I had got myself into trouble long before I met her with another lady, who had the same facility. I haven't told you about Mrs Jay. That is another story. We will come to that.

'I wished my brother Jim was over here and not in America. He was the only brother to marry — twice, bless him — and he had seen me through the Jay trouble — that was in New York days. There was no-one else I felt I could talk to. If Zibbie were alive I'd have turned to her, but I would have felt ridiculous consulting my younger sisters. And Willie wouldn't have seen my difficulty. The girls at home were anxious about me. They thought I was taking on too great a responsibility — they were so used to her medical crises when She came to stay. She had taken the Cross family over *en masse* when She was excluding the rest of the world from her confidence, even old friends. She was not satisfied to play Sir Oracle, She needed to belong in a family, to share the common experience of women and be legally married to her man.

'She was in a quandary because She was maintaining that all the best of her was buried with Lewes and that She was surrendering to my longing to look after her. I accepted that. There would have been no trouble if She observed that treaty in private, but She was dragging in what She called "human nature", and making claims for its undiscriminating appetite that I could only refute by hurting her vanity. Perhaps when we were married I could reconcile her to my prejudices. It was my only hope. I couldn't be so callous as to tell her that I made single beds a condition if we were to go on with wedding preparations. I felt such an *ass*. I can't tell you. I lost more than a stone in the weeks that followed. She went down with influenza; the attack came in useful when She was making excuses to her friends later on. She was not strictly truthful with them, giving the impression that the engagement had been only of a fortnight's duration of which half was spent in bed. We were engaged for a month. I didn't see those letters until I came to write the *Life*. I went to see her every day She was ill, ashamed of my misgivings and secret thoughts. I knew without her having to tell that what had brought on this ill-timed illness was our Oedipus conversation and her deliberate use of the word "incest", as if She was telling me to grow up and face the physical reality of what we were planning to do. My response had unnerved her. She looked at me tenderly when I called, weighed down with flowers.

' "Coming before the swallow dares," I said, apropos of the daffodils. At home that would have gone down very well, but it was always a mistake to show off before George Eliot.

' "You are a month late. You were due in March, and I am not at all sure, if you recall the rest of the quotation, that it was tactful in the circumstances."

'Then in that superb voice of hers — I wondered as I listened if the thing might not turn out all right if I kept my eyes shut and she recited Shakespeare while it was going on —

> ". . . O Proserpina!
> For the flowers now that frighted thou lets't fall
> From Dis's wagon! daffodils,
> That come before the swallow dares, and take
> The winds of March with beauty; violets dim,
> But sweeter than the lids of Juno's eyes
> Or Cytherea's breath; pale primroses,
> That die unmarried ere they can behold
> Bright Phoebus in his strength, — a malady
> Most incident to maids — "

' "Don't go on," I begged her. "I feel humiliated enough. I am out of my depth as soon as I get any distance away from my life-belts: Consols, Debentures, Three percents.''

' ''Bright Phoebus in his strength,'' she murmured; her eyes were glowing. I should have kissed her. We were an engaged couple. There was all the invitation in her eyes that a man could want. The moment passed. Then I became solicitous about her health. What had the doctor said? Was he to call again? She must conserve her energies. I asked all the usual invalid-visiting questions. ''Bright Phoebus in his strength,'' indeed!

'We never know exactly the impression we are making; I thought that I had made it clear that I was refusing to play a romantic role. Colin, I ask you to take my word, I would as soon have thought of behaving like that towards my mother. That is why the introduction of the word ''incest'' had shocked me so much, added to which having remained celibate for forty years, the idea of beginning with a woman of her age was unthinkable. Imagine my feelings when I was taking my leave and, as usual, kissed her hand when She seized one of mine, looked at me as if She was searching my soul, and said: ''I have never known any man with such self-restraint. I saw your struggle. If you had insisted I couldn't have refused you. You are the knight of legend. But you will get your reward, and perhaps it will be sweeter for having been waited for so chivalrously. I have a confession to make to you; it embarrasses me to have to. Let me rest my poor tired head on your strong shoulder. Sit here beside me, then I won't see the reproach in my knight's eye. I told you untruth. I said that I consulted Sir James about the effect our wedding would have on my influence. I mentioned this while he was here, but the reason I asked him to call was — I am glad that you can't see my face now — was because the object of his visit was to find out . . . make quite sure . . . How shall I put it? . . . Simple truth is best — and cleanest. I said that you wanted to marry me, and I asked him if my state of health would permit me to perform my wifely duties. He was quite reassuring. I should have told you this at the time. I was shy. You must forgive me. I watched you when you were relating your talk with Charles; something was upsetting you. I tried to convey to you that I am not frightened of the sex act. I lived with an understanding and considerate but very experienced man. We were always perfectly open about these matters. Can you and I not be? I see you as over-chivalrous in your attitude. Do you think I could have written my books if I had no experience of how people feel and behave? I *am* a woman first, my lover, and a writer, thinker — what you will — after that. One thing worries me. Will you regret having waited so long to marry that your bride cannot bear you a child? The age of miracles is past, and I am not Sarah. This has also saddened me. I see you lying awake in the small hours plying yourself with anxious questions. I have never been philoprogenitive; books are a writer's children, but you may well want to plant a row of Crosses."

'She was at ease, beginning to jest, comfortable in her position, all signs of influenza had disappeared. She ran her fingers through my whiskers and made as if to plait them. I stared in front of me — aghast.

'How we complicate life for ourselves by these efforts to be superior beings. I had passed beyond desperation. Here was I with the most intellectual women of her generation behaving like a romantic schoolgirl. I had been surprised by the brutality with which I had made my points, but She was determined to ignore the signals. This was how I had proposed three times: I was now holding myself back from satisfying my lustful desires. I had been praised for it: I would be praised again when She insisted that at the third time of asking I must be allowed my way.

'We were interrupted by Brett — her knock enabled me to get down from my place beside the pillow. I took the opportunity to escape. I could not face a resumption of the idyll. I am sure I would have indulged her fancies — up to the hilt I was going to say — if they had been innocent. What plagued me was the knowledge that any sign of tenderness was liable to be misinterpreted. I am sure women have this difficulty when they allow men to show affection. What a business it is!

'At my present age, Colin, when my mind entertains such thoughts — which is very rarely — I ask myself why one got so worked up about these matters? A clinical description of the process is not fetching in the least. In our efforts to dress it up we tell the most awful lies. Why was I a bachelor at forty? Because, like so many of the breed, when it came to the point I couldn't face going through the embarrassment of deflowering a virgin dressed in white for the sacrifice, and I was too fastidious to satisfy my little cravings with women who sold themselves.'

'But, surely, there were others in between, women of the world. Did you not have *affaires*? George Eliot was not the only woman to lust after you, I am quite certain.'

'Now, I wish you hadn't put it like that.'

'But I thought we were really speaking man-to-man.'

'When you use that word I feel disloyal. She was the noblest creature.'

'But, by her own confession, extremely frail and human.'

'I suppose I was lowly-sexed. I never thought much about it. I did used to wonder what women saw in some of my contemporaries who passed as Don Juans. I suppose it was simply their appetite. Women recognize it, I understand. And sympathize with it.'

'You can take it they do.'

'How is one to find out these things? I lived the life of a country curate. I see it now.'

'You were doing what you wanted. I am longing to hear the rest of the story. Did you bring the subject up again?'

'No, and I took care not to be left in a situation where I had to. I didn't know what to do. My sisters gave me tonics. I kept on muttering about worry in the office. I had to explain my loss of weight. I put on a brave face. You must understand that I was wholly devoted to her and the idea of sharing our lives was very precious to me. She made all life seem so rich and full of possibilities. Once we had got over this silly sex difficulty all would be well. We must face it and brave it, as at school, waiting for a swishing. Afterwards would be all right, the trouble behind you. But I handled it so badly, Colin. When I look back I feel so *ashamed*.'

He was looking so woe-begone at this point that I felt it would be cruel to press him further. His face was all creased up with the pouting-baby expression to which I had grown accustomed.

'I think that's all I can manage today. We had better draw stumps. I'll drop you a line when I've gone through more of my papers. I'd like to refresh this old mind of mine before we get down to business in earnest.'

Silence for a week, and no sign of Johnnie in the club, I decided that he must be ill and telephoned to inquire. That household didn't take kindly to telephones. Johnnie would push the receiver into Mrs Patterson's hands mumbling 'Tell me what he is saying.' She sounded so ferocious that it was difficult to frame a question, and she never understood what I said and said so to her employer who then took back the telephone and enquired again who was there. We went through one of these nerve-racking exchanges, but it told me he was up, and when I was putting the receiver down I heard him say, 'Tell him I have written him a letter.' He had indeed. It came next day.

Dear Colin,

You must forgive me if I seemed preoccupied after luncheon the other day. I was sorry about it particularly because my idea was that we should visit the cemetery together. I didn't feel in the mood for that. I have been much exercised about this matter between us. Loyalty to my great lady predominates, but I want someone to know the truth before I pass on. I find it increasingly difficult to live with the knowledge that I have perpetuated a lie, whatever my motive.

Since my last sister, Florence, died I have no-one I can talk to. Mrs Patterson is my sole confidante in these days of decline. And I will confess, only to you, that I have unburdened myself to her in desperation from time to time. Whenever I do, I feel remorseful. Incontinence — that, I fear, is the diagnosis; there is no effective cure at eighty-four, but I think a palliative would be if you were to undertake the book and look after publishers etc. I am past that sort of thing. I'll put all the material I have at your disposal and dictate notes that might be useful to a typist, if you haven't got shorthand. When the book is done we can look at it. If then I decide, and the decision must be mine, that it should not be published, the manuscript can be lodged in the British Museum with an embargo and I will pay you £1,000 for your trouble. If the book is published all the profits are yours, and I guarantee to make them up to the figure mentioned. If this appeals to you, tell me, and we can seal the compact at luncheon — why not? What are you doing on Thursday at one o'clock?

Your new friend,

Johnnie

III

Johnnie

FEEL DECIDEDLY GROGGY; must take the stairs nice and gently. Don't want to bring Mrs P. down on top of me. 'What are you looking for at three o'clock in the morning?' she'll be wanting to know. 'If you had asked me to I'd have brought it up to you.' She doesn't understand how you must act at once when an idea gets into your head. There is something — I'm bothered if I can remember what it is — in those diaries that I want to look at before Colin comes. I can't bring myself to just hand everything over to him. Feel I'm letting her down. But why do I feel this urge to tell it all to somebody? Don't want to be buried with my head in a bag, I suppose. Strange how the past hangs round me. Harder and harder to read newspapers. Everyone seems to be telling the same old lies, one has heard them so often, over and over again. Wouldn't mind dying now if it could be managed without too much mess — or pain. Can't stand mess, better at putting up with pain. But I won't be able to sleep if I don't get just a peep at the diaries, like looking to see if the baby is safe in his cot. Odd never to have been a father. Don't regret it much. Won't turn on the landing light. She might see it. Don't want her to catch me in the study. Don't wholly trust her. Eye on the main chance. Can't blame her really. She would talk to the nieces. Has to keep in with everyone. Could hardly keep my face straight when she read me that piece out of her newspaper about the widower who left his faithful housekeeper to the mercies of his rapacious family. She killed herself with prussic acid. Painful way to die, I'd say. Wouldn't recommend it. They let her go to the workhouse. I acted stupid, asking where precisely the workhouse was, as if that were the point of the story. I saw her eye on the poker. The way the stairs creak. Never notice it in daylight.

Fire not quite out. Good. With a little poking I'll get it going again. Don't have to look for the diaries — staring at me from the book case since . . . forty-four years? Can it be so long? Damn silly locking them in there and leaving the key in the lock. But I like to keep my books behind glass. Terrible dust-collectors. Won't trust anyone except myself to clean them. I'll put the diaries on the sofa table and sit close to the fire. It won't take long.

'Are you all right, Sir? What a screech you gave. What has you down here at this hour of night?'

'Look at this Mrs Patterson. My wife's diaries, mutilated. All the early years torn out by some ruffian. This is the worst thing that has ever happened to me. I'm going to get to the bottom of this; no-one except myself has the right to go to that book-case.'

'No-one goes near it except yourself. I thought someone must have cut your throat.'

'But do you realize, it's manuscript — her own handwriting; and there isn't a copy in the world. This is terrible.'

'Those books have been sitting up there for as long as I've known you. This might have happened years ago, long before my time. If you would get back to your bed I'll heat up some milk for you. You'll be getting your death of cold if you stay down here.'

I let her shepherd me upstairs, fussing and complaining over her shoulder with all the tiresomeness of her class. There is nothing else I could do at this hour. I am sorely tempted to ring Colin up but resist the impulse. He wouldn't thank me, not at this time of night. Thank goodness he is coming tomorrow. I want to talk to him. He might have some valuable suggestion to make.

'Your bottle is cold. I'll heat it up for you.'

'Thank you, Mrs Patterson.'

Now I have a chance to think. When was the last time I looked at the diaries? Writing the *Life*; they were the first source I turned to, but I didn't use much of the early part. It upset me. She was in a morbid state of mind at the time and too much alone (and abroad at that). I 'forgot' a great deal for my own peace of mind, and I declare to goodness, I don't think I've glanced at them since. She was looking very hard at life. With her father's death She had lost what She described in some letter I saw as 'that purifying restraining influence' and without him She had a 'horrid vision' of herself becoming 'earthly, sensual and devilish'. Utter rubbish, of course; but who was to tell her?

Did I ever look at the diaries since? I couldn't say. My memory has become so treacherous lately. Perhaps I haven't. It's perfectly possible. Anything I wanted was in the *Life*. Forty-four years is a long time, and I've moved house pretty often since then. Anyone might have got hold of them. A clean sweep of all the early pages. What a monstrous thing to do.

'Now that is very kind of you Mrs Patterson. I am very sorry for giving so much trouble. I got quite a start, I must tell you.'

'You woke the house up. I don't know what they must be thinking next door.'

'I'm very sorry, but it was the worst fright I have ever had. Exactly like something in a bad dream. And, you know, it couldn't have happened at a more unfortunate time. I wanted to refresh my memory before Colin — Mr Cathcart comes. He is going to write the new *Life* of my wife. I haven't told you about my plan, have I? I didn't want to until I had quite made up my mind that he was the right person. I want him to work here as much as possible. I couldn't get to sleep for the life of me. The book was so much in my head.'

'But have you taken leave of your senses? You wrote your wife's *Life*. Why would you ask someone to come in off the street and write it all over again? That's what I call mad behaviour.'

'I didn't do it very well, and Mr Cathcart is an excellent writer, not just someone from off the street by any means. Someone else will do it some day if he doesn't. I thought it might be fun to see it started while I was still around. I have very little to interest me these days, you know. I can't get accustomed to the wireless. It's like listening to mice in the wainscot. Anyhow, that's not the point. I thought I would refresh my memory about a certain matter, and I got up to look if it was in the diaries. I can't remember what's in them and what's in letters people lent me. It is all mixed together in my mind after around forty or more years. I wanted to be ready for him. He is very keen. What am I going to do now?'

'Are you sure the diaries weren't always like that?'

'With pages torn out? All the early part? Certainly not. My memory may be bad, but I would remember that. I'm dreadfully worried. I'd be much obliged to you if you would ring Mr Cathcart first thing in the morning and ask him to look in during the day. You'll find his telephone number under "Colin" on my pad.'

Mrs. Patterson is becoming very difficult lately. I spoil her. It's hard not to when one becomes as dependent on anyone as I am on her. Knows all my ways, and having been so long with Anna makes her like one of the family. Better be careful; and not say *that* again. Went down very badly when I let it slip out last time the Druces were here. The nieces find it hard to be civil to her. They can't suspect her of having designs on me! It's too absurd. Really! But I do see how an unscrupulous woman in her position could put the pressure on by threatening to leave one in the lurch. They all *say* they would love to take me in, but it wouldn't be long before they'd be finding me a damn nuisance. Nobody wants the old. Wonder if it would put their minds at ease if I were to tell them about my will. *She* would have. It was her idea that we should make our wills immediately after the wedding. But then She had a no-nonsense attitude towards money. Can't have a bailiff as a father and generations of carpenters in the blood and entertain fanciful notions about LSD. She told everyone that I had my own fortune, and no expectations from her. Funny thing to do, I thought at the time. She must have wanted to shut up anyone who might suggest I had married her for her money. She was so terribly embarrassed about the whole business. When I used to tell her about my own family's ups and downs of fortune, She liked to smile. Nothing ever happened to us that a retreat to Brighton or a few years abroad couldn't mend, but when She went to Germany with Lewes — he had a wife and children to support — they often dined off bread and dripping. For years — until She wrote the novels — She had no frock fit to wear in the evening.

I wonder how much whisky Mrs P. put into the milk. Feel as drunk as an owl.

IV

Colin

Belgravia is off my usual beat, and as I approached Chester Square, having taken the underground to Victoria, I was glad that I had first encountered Johnnie away from his home ground. His reference to his circumstances had not prepared me for such stuccoed splendour, four storeys, with attics above and basements below. No. 88, when I came to it, was off the square in a row of houses as tall but narrower than those in the square proper, and the stucco stopped at street level. There was a balcony over the door.

Mrs P. — it could be none other — vinegar-blooded, knife-faced, let me in. I thought I heard keys rattle, but my imagination may have been playing tricks on me. I expected a chilly welcome, but this morning, at least, she seemed to be pleased to see me.

'How is he?'

'All excited, just what the doctor told him not to be. I'd like to have a word with you, Mr Cathcart, before you go upstairs.' She led me into the study and shut the door, but did not invite me to sit down. She was full of importance. I thought of a court martial. It would begin like this. 'I heard this shriek in the night and thought someone was being murdered. I looked into his room but he wasn't there, but there was a light on in the study downstairs, so I armed myself with a poker and went in. You could have knocked me down with a feather. There he was, curled up on the sofa, crying like a child. He had come down in the night to look at his missus's diaries. He usually keeps them in the book case over there. I asked him what the matter was, and he said someone had been tearing pages out of his wife's diaries. I said no-one would do the like of that, and I hoped he was not making any reflections on anyone in the house. Of course there are these people who come from time to time pretending to be admirers of

George Eliot on the look-out for what they can get out of him. He has become very silly lately; you must have noticed it yourself, sir.

'He has this idea that there is someone called Strachey on his tracks who wants to make mischief, if you know what I mean. I don't know what has got into him. This Strachey fellow, whoever he is, must know it. I think myself it's the Master's age is beginning to show. Old people get strange fancies into their heads. In my opinion the diaries — exercise books I call them — are in the same state as they have always been, certainly since I have been here. Who would want to go tearing pages out of them? Unless it was a ghost. Don't stay with him too long. He got very little sleep last night. The doctor said he was to avoid excitement.'

'Where are the diaries now?'

'Up in his room. He won't let them out of his sight.'

'Ah, Colin.'

My old friend looked rather flushed, I thought, and his eager greeting reminded me of a boy busy at a game, too concentrated on it to look up as he invites you to join in. Lying on the bed were what I assumed to be the diaries.

'You've heard what happened? Mrs P. told you? It was very good of you to come round so promptly. It really was a shock. Let me show you. Those later ones seem to be all right, but look here: all the early diary is torn out, from the time her father died until she started to live with Lewes. All that crucial period in the fifties when she worked on the *Westminster Review* under Chapman is gone, her friendship with Spencer, her first meeting with Lewes. We don't need the later stuff.

'Lewes recorded all that. I hope Mrs P. didn't get the impression I suspected her. She is convinced it must be the work of the Welshman who borrowed an umbrella of mine and didn't return it. I wish I could remember when I last looked at them. You will hardly credit it, but I may well not have since I used them for the book. That's a long time ago, and they have had many homes in the interval. I kept a house at Tonbridge for years when I was living with my widowed sister Anna Druce. Anyone might have got at them there. I was never one to do much locking-up.'

'You don't suspect anyone?'

'Who, I ask myself, had a motive? I can only think of two people, Herbert Spencer and George Chapman.'

'Both dead?'

'Oh, yes. A long time.'

'Then I think you must try to forget about it . As soon as you feel well enough I think we should have a session about where there may be letters that for various reasons you didn't get a chance to see when you were writing the biography. No-one who had George Eliot letters would destroy them. I thought we might begin with a letter to *The Times Literary Supplement.* We can talk about that later on. I called just to see how you were.'

'You got my letter?'

'I did indeed.'

'And you are happy about that?'

'It sounds very satisfactory. There are a few details I would like to discuss when you are better, but in principle you may take it I am your man.'

'But this set-back at the very start; I must say I find it most discouraging.'

'There should be unpublished letters to make up for the loss of the diary. If She was abroad alone, I'm sure She poured her soul out to someone.'

He refused to take comfort. Was he, it suddenly occurred to me, playing up this diary loss as yet another excuse for evading the issue? I was as vague as ever about the kind of book he wanted me to write, but I was no longer wasting my time. I had sold him that. Mrs P. was waiting for me in the hall.

'How do you think he is?'

'Much better than I expected. Has he told you that I am going to be haunting the house from now on?'

The closest approximation to a smile I had seen so far, like the first crack in a long-frozen pond, broke the mask of disapproval that Mrs P. habitually wore, not because she was necessarily feeling critical of what was going forward at the moment but to make sure she wouldn't be caught when she did, like the foolish virgins, unprepared.

'You *are* going to write the book. Well, that ought to please him. He was hoping you would. He can't talk about anything else since the idea came into his head.'

'I'm sorry he had this shock at the beginning.'

'About them diaries?'

'Exactly.'

'If I was you, I wouldn't be worrying my head too much about them. It's my belief he tore those pages out himself and forgot about it after. His memory plays him strange tricks lately. You are coming to lunch tomorrow. We will expect you around one. Don't let him get too excited, whatever you do. We don't want a repeat of last night. My nerves wouldn't stand it.'

Laura's phone had been out of order, otherwise I would have told her about Johnnie's offer. He was giving us the cash injection we needed — £1,000 seemed like a great deal of money in 1924; we could afford to get married. Laura would help me in innumerable ways — she had an Edinburgh degree with all that implied of a no-nonsense approach to her work, nicely calculated to restrain my tendency to start unlikely hares. I waited until I had clinched the deal to tell her the good news. It looked better as a *fait accompli* than a mere suggestion: my trouble was that I had given Laura a frivolous impression of my patron. Her sense of humour is less attuned to the absurd than mine is. She has no time for facetiousness. I could see now how much damage I had done my cause by referring to Johnnie as the Ancient Mariner. She saw him as a waste of time, a joke figure. One side of me was unworthily looking forward to a gloat; in spite of her disapproval I had struck oil. The better side of my nature was simply delighted to be telling her that nest-making preparations could begin at once. And I was anxious to persuade a girl who was giving up a post to marry me that she was on to a good thing.

I spoke rather fast, trying to get all the good side in before any snags appeared. She was pleased and excited. I didn't gloat (except inwardly) but when I went on to tell about the Great Diary Robbery, the note of rhapsody in her voice died away. She took the vandalism to the diaries in her stride; what upset her was when I chortled over Mrs P.'s idea that he had been the culprit. It wasn't out of the question by any means; if he didn't think the news was fit to print at the time he might well have decided not to leave it lying about.

'I'd insist on a reasonable advance,' Laura said. 'What would happen if after a few months you found him impossible to get on with?'

'And he might die?'

'Anything might happen. I wish I had more faith in the project.' It was my turn to feel dejected. I could see Laura having qualms; next thing she would be suggesting a halt to the marriage plans until the money was in my pocket. I must prevent this.

'I tell you what — if I can get Johnnie to part with half the cash now and the balance when the book is completed or in, say, eighteen months if the delay is no fault of mine — would you feel safer then?'

'Anyone would. But do you think he will agree? He sounds to me a highly unpredictable old buffer.'

'I'll do my damnedest, and when I lodge that cheque in our joint account, may I have your permission to apply for a licence?'

'A licence to do what?'

I liked the sound of her voice just then. It stiffened my determination. I would stand no nonsense from Johnnie. This was the most eventful decision I had made in my life so far.

I sat down then and wrote a letter formally accepting the offer and explaining my own position. I couldn't leave my fiancée uncertain about our plans. I needed the wherewithal to marry and I could not spend more than eighteen months on the task. As a banker he would know how to make out the manner of payment. He could rely on me to concentrate exclusively on the task. Presumably there would be a certain amount of travelling to do. Could I depend on him to defray the cost? It is extraordinary what love will do; I had never written such a Shylock letter to anyone. I conjured up Laura in the background urging me on. She is tougher than I am.

He came out of his study to greet me in the hall when I called next morning. Mrs P. shooed him back out of the draught.

'He has been listening all morning for your knock.' She had a way of talking about him as if he couldn't hear, which he never seemed to mind.

A table in the study was loaded with books and papers; I was touched by two blotters, silver ink pots and pen trays laid out as if we were going to eat a meal with them.

The letter in my pocket was poking me in the ribs. How was I going to present it? My employer was in no hurry. Contemplating the feast on the table was obviously all he required at the moment. Once again I had misgivings: was he proposing to buy my time and attention? The Ancient Mariner never thought of this. Much as I liked the prospect of a large advance — £50 was the best I had succeeded in extracting from my publishers so far — I would not prostitute myself. Laura would be highly contemptuous of the notion. It would be an unworthy start to our life together.

I cleared my throat. 'I think I should give you my acceptance of your terms. I have a few qualifications to make. Perhaps you should read them before we begin.'

'Whatever you say. I'm perfectly happy.'

He ran a remarkably quick eye over the letter which had cost me such exquisite pain to compose. 'I'll give you a cheque for the whole amount now, and if you get anything from the publishers eventually, hold on to it. My cheque book is over there on the desk. Hand it to me like a good fellow.'

'I didn't mean —'

'Let's get the money out of the way. You must bring — what's your lady's name?'

'Laura.'

'Laura to see me. I daresay she comes to London sometimes.' He seemed to enjoy filling in the cheque. 'That's done. Put that in your pocket. Now, where do we begin?' It was the moment I had been waiting for. I wanted to say, 'Let's begin in Venice. We can work backwards.' Under the new dispensation, there need be no beating about this or any other bushes. I hesitated. Fatal.

'Look at the diary. You can see how the early years have been torn out. I shall try to recollect what I can. It is important. Unless you know how her mind worked in those years before she knew me you can't see our problem in perspective.'

The diary had been savagely attacked by someone. We would have to begin by looking at how much of it he had used in the *Life* (a copy of the one-volume edition lay like a side plate beside our blotters). 'What is your plan? A new biography — that would take years if we were to do it properly. I had in mind something in the nature of a journal of your friendship and marriage. It is up to you how candid you wish to be about the central problem. If you don't meet it head on, there doesn't seem to be much point in the exercise.'

'Certainly, but I don't want to appear a muff. In fairness to myself I should be allowed to explain that the George Eliot of legend (partly my own invention, I agree) was in reality a highly-strung, passionate woman who got herself deeply involved with every man She came in contact with. That is the truth. I speak it in my own defence. Take Spencer, for instance. She threw herself at him. Admittedly She was too honest to resort to flirtatious wiles, and these were not at her disposal. The first view of her was not alluring, and as a young woman She hadn't developed into the charmer that She became when She was sure of herself and knew her own worth. Then She could make the most of her assets, her lovely voice, her pianist's hands, her ability to concentrate her attention. When she arrived in London She was an opinionated, gawky young woman with a sad awareness of her physical defects and a longing for a suitable man who would be all in all to her. She found him in Lewes eventually. When Lewes died She was lost. She had forgotten how to live alone. I had three recommendations: I was free to marry, a reasonable male specimen, and with a family background of the kind She appreciated. She put the family first among human blessings.

'Now, trace her history: She very nearly marries a picture-restorer when She is in her twenties; She is asked to leave Doctor Brabant's house by his wife; She dotes on the married Chapman; She makes a one-sided declaration of love to Herbert Spencer; She goes off with the married Lewes, and She ends up at sixty with a husband nearly half her age. That is not the curriculum vitae of Mrs Grundy. And yet this woman was a strong moral force, a great and generous human being. Lady Paget, the surgeon's wife, said she was jealous of George Eliot's hold over her husband; even the epicene Henry James said he was in love with her, which in his case meant that he could conceive of one of his fictional heroes falling in love with her. That is the woman you are dealing with. Of course, She was a genius.'

'You think then that Spencer may have got at the diary?'

'Certainly not. Spencer was a gentleman — well, more or less. Chapman was another kettle of fish. You won't find him under his own name in the index. The man was a blackguard and an impostor. If I could have avoided mentioning his name in connection with her, I would have. He took her on to help him edit the *Westminster Review*. He wasn't up to it. His role was to hold weekly soirées in his office in the Strand. It was at these that my wife met Spencer and Lewes and became part of the London literary world. Before that She was a provincial with awkward manners and no clothes to wear at parties. Not that She was any better off in the article of cash. Chapman exploited her. In the end She was working for him for nothing.'

'But why?'

'Because She was besotted with him, my dear boy. I read it in her diary and even there I could see She did not tell the whole story.'

'Here he paused in full career and, lowering his voice, "Make sure no-one is listening there,' nodding in the direction of the door. This is something I associated with melodramas. In real life I wasn't sure how one went about it. Supposing Mrs P. did have her ear at the key-hole — what then? Better not to discover her, I'd have thought. I made as much noise as possible crossing the room and opened the door very slowly.

'Coast clear?'

I nodded, and came back to my seat.

'Servants gossip. I don't want this to go any further. You understand? It is what worries me about your book. If I could be sure there was no other evidence I really think we should suppress this. Chapman had extensive premises in the Strand and made ends meet by taking in highbrow lodgers. He had a wife, older than himself, whom he had married for her money and a governess for the children who was his mistress. That is the ménage the strictly-reared country girl found herself in.'

'She probably didn't know what was going on.'

'She did. That's the amazing thing. The three women were at loggerheads within a few days of her arrival. Chapman was the cock of the walk. He kept all three in play. Finally wife and mistress joined forces and said they wanted Miss Evans out. Mrs Chapman had caught them holding hands. He used to spend hours in her room. She played the piano for him and gave him Greek lessons. You can imagine my feelings, Colin dear, when I read that and thought of our Dante-worshipping sessions. It was a watershed in my life.'

'What happened?'

'To me?'

'To the Chapman friendship.'

'Oh, there was a sad entry about a farewell at the railway station. She asked Chapman if he loved her and he said he did, in her way; but he loved his wife, in her way, and the governess, in her way. So there was not much comfort in that.'

'She was well rid of him.'

'But she wasn't. Chapman couldn't afford to lose her. He was an utter charlatan. He found another London lodging for her, and they swore a pact of platonic friendship and made peace with the ladies and She went on working for him for nothing.'

'He must have had . . .'

'Oh, the ladies loved him. In no time he had Barbara Bodichon — Leigh Smith as she was then — in my dearest's place. They planned to have a baby but thought better of it.'

'This is a strange insight into Victorian domestic life.'

'You can imagine the impression that it made on me. What upset me most were those Greek lessons. I went through a bad time. My faith, you might say, was tested. I was greatly helped by the thought of Mother and my sisters. They had instilled respect for women into me. I held on to it.'

'But I don't suppose the worst happened. Do you?'

'No. No. Of course not.'

There was a silence then, which I was first to break.

'So far as I can remember, George Eliot went away with Lewes not long after the time we are talking about.'

'About a year later. First She was inseparable from Spencer, then he introduced her to Lewes, and within a few months they went away to Germany together. He was finishing his Goethe book. She helped him with it.'

'There was always a man in her life?'

'Not at the beginning. She had an hysterical fit at her first party. I believe it was brought on by her conviction that She was too ugly to attract a man. She was haunted by her plain face. It exasperated her to find, however She tried to keep up with fashion, nothing helped it. She was very feminine, always asking my sisters to buy her ribbons and laces; the problem of keeping up drawers exercised her mind.'

'Did She solve it?'

'Yes. Made herself braces.'

Mrs P., whether she had been listening or not, now decided that I had stayed too long. She came in to say Doctor Benn was on his way. It would not do if he was to discover me with his patient.

'Damn Dr Benn. We were only just beginning to get somewhere. Could we continue this tomorrow, Colin?'

'It did not suit my plans, but I was determined to take advantage of Johnnie's new expansive mood. At any moment he might go back to evasive tactics. I thought I understood these swinging changes: there was a delicately poised balance — likely to tip over at any moment — between the senile urge to make himself as interesting to someone else as he was to himself (he thought about nothing but himself in the past) and, in the other scale, various inhibitions, loyalty, the sacredness of secrets etc.

This see-sawing explained the diary mystery; Mrs P. had known him longer than I had. He was muddled. He tore pages out in one of his downswings. The excitement at eighty-four of throwing off Mother's influence had gone to his head. He was questioning whether George Eliot was the plaster saint he had insisted She was. I assumed She had kept a discreet silence about several matters. Brooding over them to brief me he might well have had an impulse to check what was in the diary to see how much he had left out or fudged to show the world a picture of womanly perfection. I could see that he was more than a little uneasy about his three alleged proposals of marriage. He knew that he hadn't made them; a climate had been established in which She decided what was in his mind by the light of her vastly superior intelligence. Spencer had paid tribute to her intellect; he had also credited her with an imagination on the same scale. Johnnie was beginning to suspect not all of it went into her novels. She belonged I could see with the women who do nothing by halves, for whom the idea of flirtation is inconceivable. They are highly inflammable and, in my experience, usually on the plain side. I wished Laura were here. I would like to discuss all this with her. Mrs P. told me she was giving him a sedative. I hoped it would not have the effect of changing his present mood. I could see that the most effective role for me to adopt to achieve my purpose would be to play Iago to his Othello. Or would he insist he was a willing victim? We still hadn't got to Venice, and that was, for me, the whole point of the story. But I knew there was nothing to be achieved by not listening patiently to the lost diary mystery. One thing at a time.

'He seems better in himself today,' Mrs P. said when I arrived next morning. 'I could hardly get him to finish his breakfast he is that excited. He was up at all hours, insisted on coming down. Don't let him exhaust himself.'

Johnnie, newly shaved, in a paisley dressing-gown and white silk scarf, looked like an advertisement for life assurance. His manners were always perfect. He must have chafed at the waste of time enquiring about my journey on the bus, hoping he wasn't encroaching too much on my time etc. I had to rescue him from his old-fashioned courtesy. With patent relief that duty had been done he started on what I recognized at once as the pursuit of a hare.

'Does the name Brabant strike a chord?'

'You let his name drop.'

'He is certainly worth mentioning. George Eliot got the idea of Casaubon from him.'

'I thought —'

'Everyone gets it wrong. Brabant was a doctor who lived at Devizes. He was by the way of writing a vast tome to disprove once and for all the divinity of Christ, but never got beyond the opening chapter. He left bundles and bundles of indecipherable notes behind him. A charlatan. She got her revenge, don't you think? Although She used to say in sport that Casaubon was the unsleeping pedant in herself that was forever trying to bury the artist under his sawdust.'

'But why did She want to take revenge? What had Dr Brabant done?'

'That's something else that I meant to look for in the diaries. I got the outlines from her Coventry friends. I made no reference to him in the *Life*, but I perceive that he provided a key. I am beginning to see a pattern.'

'I am fascinated.'

He bowed gratefully, not detecting the note of resignation in my voice. We seemed to be travelling in the wrong direction. I cursed myself for having upset my plans for the day.

'You won't find Brabant in my index. His daughter's name appears. When she got married to one of my dear one's Coventry friends, she handed over to her the translating of Strauss's *Life of Jesus*. I wouldn't have thanked her for it. Grim work. Wretched pay. However, Dr Brabant met Mary Anne — She wasn't George Eliot then — at the wedding. She was a bridesmaid. He was so taken with her that he issued an invitation straight away. She was to come to Devizes to take his daughter's place and console him, and stay a month.'

'How old was he?'

'Sixty-three. She accepted at once. I suppose She got her stern father's permission. But She was a big girl now.'

'Rather precipitate of the old gentleman. Did Mrs Brabant object?'

'In a letter to one of her Coventry friends, She described her hostess as "perfectly polite". I remember the impression that "perfectly polite" made on me when I read it. It was the one drab note in a lyrical picture of life at Devizes; She was being coddled —'

'What did you say?'

'Coddled, and petted and fussed over, and walking and talking and reading with her father-substitute, and having luxurious feelings of faintness, which meant lying on sofas and even more fussing over her. She was enjoying it so much that She was writing to her father for permission to extend the month to six weeks.'

'Do we know what part Mrs Brabant took in the celebrations?'

'None at all. She couldn't take any.'

'Why not?'

'She was stone blind. Her sister who lived with them must have taken an unsympathetic view of the performance. After the third day she spelled out the quickest route from Devizes to

Coventry for the visitor's benefit.'

'That was rather pointed.'

'Brabant must have told her to take no notice. When the bride came home she took a poor view of the situation, but whether or not she encouraged her aunt to upset the apple-cart, I could never find out.'

'Encouraged her aunt to do what?'

'Speak to her mother. Whatever she said to her, Mrs Brabant ordered my darling to go home. If She didn't, she said, she would leave herself.'

'And what did the Doctor say?'

'He followed Adam's example in a similar crisis.'

'Let her down.'

'Precisely. Said it was her fault. She never held it against him. Not in my hearing anyhow. And She can't have complained because he invited her to join a party going to Germany a few years later. She didn't accept the invitation. She used to say Brabant never took her in for a second. He was only helping her to pass the time. It was a low point in her career.'

'Before Chapman?'

'Before Chapman.'

Mention of that name seemed to depress him. But I was trying to get the conversation back on the rails. Brabant was a foot-note.

'She suffered such beastly humiliations. I didn't know about them until the last few weeks of our marriage.'

'After Venice?'

'After Venice, as you say. She fell into a very reminiscent vein. She told me many things that I believe She had been brooding over and wanted to release before She went. I think She knew She was travelling towards death.'

I pretended not to see Johnnie struggling with tears. He had been as perky as I had ever seen him until I mentioned Chapman.

'You did everything a man could. You have nothing to reproach yourself with. She must have had an incurable condition.'

'I could have given her a fuller life, a renewal. I failed her. I was one more on the list of her inadequate men. No. That is unfair. I must except Lewes. Lewes could not have been more devoted, but he was an extraordinary little man to look at, like a performing monkey and, then, he was never in a position to marry her. For all her attempts to justify her position, She grieved over the fact that She wasn't Mrs Lewes. Nothing offended her more than to see herself described as anything else on an envelope. I went through a painful time with her after Lewes died when the Court insisted that She be described as "Mary Anne Evans, Spinster" on the probate papers.'

'It doesn't matter now.'

'But I want to do her justice. I want you to write a truly great biography. We can't expect to make another Boswell out of you, but there are other precedents. Your book must supersede my misjudged but well-intentioned effort and bring George Eliot back.'

'As Strachey brought back Queen Victoria.'

'Strachey be damned. Victoria be damned. What possessed you to produce that comparison? Have I been mistaken in my choice? It is to save her from that blackguard with his obscene beard I took you on in the first place.'

'A slip of the tongue. I wasn't thinking about what I was saying.'

'I should hope not.'

He was quite put out. There was nothing I could do. When I asked him questions he gave me short dry answers. I cursed myself for my gaffe and bided my time. When he yawned twice and apologized, I pleaded the engagement I had cancelled as an excuse to leave. I was kicking myself. Strachey's name was enough to spoil his day — I knew that — how could I have been so tactless? It was the measure of my despair at the idea of yet another marathon biography. What I had in mind was something like the elegant short biographies Maurois was writing. If only I had had the wit to give *him* as an example. I said 'Strachey' because I meant Strachey: this was material of which he would have made marvellous use. If Johnnie could have seen into my mind I would have been dismissed on the spot. I wrote a letter of apology that evening and urged him to consider the possibility of a book which, instead of going over the ground again, was confined to the time of his marriage, when he required no other witness. *Story of a Marriage*, I suggested as the title. The world had not heard enough about the man George Eliot married. It was a moving story; people would like to hear about it; he had stayed in the shadows for far too long.

I rang up religiously every day to enquire for him, to be assured by Mrs P. that he was much recovered but taking things easy. I began to wonder whether my clumsiness had put an end to our enterprise when a fat envelope arrived in the post in the familiar handwriting, tremulous copper-plate. I put it unopened in my pocket. It would have to be studied at leisure. I still wonder what prevented me from looking to see if sentence of banishment had been passed on me.

'Dear Boy,' it began. 'You should not have chosen that moment to introduce the name of the wretch, but you could not have known that I was already upset; our tour of the past had brought back many unhappy recollections. I felt disloyal after I told you the Brabant story: it demonstrates one of her characteristics, the way She had of taking people over. She did not care for general conversation. Even when She and Lewes entertained the world (if not always his wife) She used to sit apart from the company with a chair beside her to which you were brought for a private audience. I am reminded of the scene in churches abroad when I see confessionals. In her early days this too-muchness of manner had the appearance of taking over other women's husbands. She had a large personality and a passion for *tête-à-tête*. You made some passing reference to her need of men. It was true inasmuch as She desperately needed a permanent life *à deux*; She had a compulsion to share. It explained her readiness to discuss the state of her health and to listen to the state of yours, a trait which did nothing to heighten the charm of her correspondence. In her evangelistic, provincial youth, as an awkward, plain-featured girl, convinced that her ugliness would keep suitors at bay, She must be

nature — I can imagine it. No doubt he had used it in similar situations before and was satisfied to look after the sounds and let the sense look after itself. Can you picture them? He in love only with himself; She resting her chin in her hand, elbow on the ground, fascinated by his profile, not listening very hard, but with ears pricked for any note of encouragement; in high spirits, remember, plans for London have been fixed. Then he goes on with his al fresco sermon. Everything that is marvellous, beautiful and mysterious in nature is seen at its most marvellous, most beautiful and most mysterious when it is brought together and realized in man and woman. The junction of these is life at its most beautiful — or words to that effect (he was a specious ruffian). She looked at him, so confident in his good looks, and thought of her own ugliness. It was too much. She started to sob.

'I have always hated Chapman since She described that day of disappointment. But in the process of looking back — and that has been my sole occupation since our talks began — I find my own complacency crumbling: to what extent did I offend by treating her as a cathedral instead of a woman? She said to me once that I had been ruined for other women by my mother. At the time I accepted this as a tribute and read nothing critical in the remark. But I have lately been thinking very hard about those few months of marriage, and I see where I failed her, and with more serious results than any wounds to her vanity that Chapman may have inflicted. I was ill when we married. A man can't help that. I try to console myself, but I am haunted by what I now see as her decision to die. The gods gave her everything except a pretty face. There were moments when She would have given them back all their gifts to know for twenty-four hours what it was like to look at the world from behind one. We were never closer — don't misunderstand me — than in those weeks after Venice, when my health recovered and hers declined. She told me many of her secrets. I thought we were in perfect harmony but there was always, I now believe, a bitterness at fate behind her apparent serenity. I caught a glimpse of it one day when we were staying with my brother-in-law and the Jebbs came to dinner. Jebb, I should mention, was a distinguished Cambridge classicist, and always delighted to talk to George Eliot; his vivacious American wife made much of me. I met my own wife's eye. There was anguish in it, and I noticed a distinct shortness in her manner when she talked afterwards to Lady Jebb. She hated being older than us all. What could I do? I felt a little impatient as well as deeply sympathetic. I had offered her my devotion unconditionally, but there were unalterable facts. The disparity in our ages was one.

'I would like to discuss the significance of that remark about my mother having spoiled me for other women. I was under the impression she had trained me for my role as George Eliot's husband and handed me over when she died. I wouldn't have married anyone so long as Mother was alive and needed me.

'I am bothered and puzzled by many questions. Please call soon, and don't, I beg you, mention the name of *that person*.

As ever,

Johnnie'

I had been visiting friends in Ebury Street, and as I came out of their hotel I thought of Johnnie. Chester Square was close at hand, and as I always felt inhibited about telephoning to that house, I decided to make a call; it was another opportunity to see Johnnie at home.

A housemaid answered my knock, but before I had completed my introduction of myself Mrs P. swooped down on us and took over. Mr Cross, she assured me, was very well but in bed with a cough; he was inclined to catch colds at this time of year. She must have assumed that my presence would be welcome because I was led upstairs without delay. From the back there was something of the prison wardress about her, and I wondered whether this was natural or acquired.

'Here's a visitor for you,' she said.

He was looking more than usually like a well-bathed baby today, propped up on pillows, in broad-striped flannel pyjamas.

'Colin! My dear fellow; what a delightful surprise.'

'I was in Ebury Street and I couldn't find myself so close without dropping in to see how you were.'

'Tip top. Never better. I'm nursing a ghost of a cough to make quite sure I'll be fit and well for you on Sunday. I haven't been in Ebury Street for ages. I can't go without running into George Moore, who never loses a chance to say something disagreeable, so I decided to keep out of his way. Pull in that comfortable chair and sit yourself down. Mrs P. will bring up some refreshment. She doesn't wait to be told.'

(In a few minutes she came in with a silver tray on which there were a decanter of madeira, thin biscuits on a Worcester plate and two glasses of white port.)

'This is only a morning call. I shall have to be on my way in a minute. I wanted just to see how you were.'

'I will keep off *the* subject, I promise you. That is for Sunday. I think you must often dread the sight of me. Always on to the same topic, but you see I do think of other things. I was reading *Vanity Fair* when you came in. I must know it almost by heart. What a masterpiece!'

Rashly I enquired what George Eliot thought of Thackeray.

It was madness when I was on a flying visit. The mention of that name was all that was ever needed to release the torrent. 'She disliked his cynicism, but She didn't read much by her contemporaries — a little Trollope and She had a great addiction to Anny Thackeray's novels. No-one reads them nowadays, I suppose. It's odd that you should bring up the subject because I have been thinking a lot about Anny lately. Do you remember my telling you that G.E. said I proposed to her three times? Whenever I have nothing else to think about I wonder what gave her that impression. I fly all over the ground trying to pick out what She mistook — the dear — for camouflaged proposals. I believe Anny Thackeray was responsible for one of them.'

He had settled himself even more comfortably into his pillows and given his great bottom a corresponding jerk under the bed-clothes; his eyes were half-shut. He had become oblivious to everything but the intoxication of a reminiscent flow.

I stood up. 'We must go into that on Sunday; I'm longing to hear the story, but I must be in the Strand before one.'

'Sit where you are, this won't take a moment, and by the next time I see you I shall probably have forgotten about it. You know that Anny married Richmond Ritchie when she was forty and he was coming down from Cambridge? She could have been his mother. Lewes was alive at the time, but he was dead when they had their first child; that marriage was a subject of endless interest to George Eliot. She was forever talking about it and praising them for ignoring family opposition, holding the Ritchies up as an example of what marriage should be. She saw a lot of Anny and enjoyed her funny zany ways. She told my dear one that what precipitated the wedding was her solemn brother-in-law Leslie Stephen's coming into the drawing-room unannounced and finding the lovers kissing.

'At the time I thought She went on too much about the Ritchies — they were not as fascinating to me as She seemed to find them. My reluctance irked her; She kept on raising the subject. Sometimes it became a bore, but I read nothing else into it. What a greenhorn I was. One day She challenged me: if I had been in Ritchie's shoes would I have married Anny?

' "Yes, if I truly loved her. I certainly hope so."

' "Can't you do better than that, young man?"

' "I see how his family might have discouraged him. The huge discrepancy between their ages was a bit of a facer. I have to acknowledge that."

' "But you would agree that he was going to marry someone quite out of the ordinary. If suitability of age were the criterion his family could have brought him girls in shoals to select from."

' "I am not a good person to ask. If it hadn't been for family pressure I'd have married Anna Jay."

' "How much older than you was *Anna Jay*, if I may be so bold as to ask?"

'The deep organ peal of that *Anna Jay*, the tragic intensity She lent to that rather homely name was quite alarming.

' "She was ten years younger than me."

' ''Younger!''

'My goodness, how relieved She looked. I saw her press her heart. I was mystified; it never occurred to me that She might be thinking about us.

' ''Don't misunderstand me. No-one attaches more importance to the family than I do. When Mr Lewes and I made our great decision I was quite prepared — although sad, of course — to suffer any harm to old friendships; what I found very hard to bear was the disapproval of my own family, my brother's in particular. So, don't think that I belittle your concern for family unity. If you wanted to marry the wise course would have been to introduce your bride-to-be to the circle and let them assimilate her merits gradually, not to thrust her upon them as you must have Anna Jay when they were unprepared and could see only the obvious discrepancies. I think your family is the most complete unit of its kind I know. Our model family, Mr Lewes used to say, and it expands its embrace so graciously to take in each new set of in-laws — Halls, Otters, Druces. The circle is always complete yet always capable of expansion. You saw our tribute to the Crosses when we adopted you all as nephews and nieces. I could never feel that I was merely with friends when I stayed at Weybridge. You all, including your sweet mother, gave us the impression that we were honorary life members.''

' ''As indeed you were.''

' ''*Were*?''

'I wish I could be Henry Irving for a moment to give you some impression of the tragic solemnity She gave to that *were*. In a play the gates of Heaven would be closing behind her as She was speaking. I knew of old that this high drama would be followed by hysteria, and unless I was callous there was only one way of averting that.

' ''*Are*, and always will be. You are at the very centre of their affections.''

' ''*Their*, did I hear you say?''

' ''I thought that by this time you had come to realize my chief aim in life is to promote your happiness.''

' ''That is unequivocal? You ask for no latitude?''

' ''None.''

' ''Give me time to digest this. He is still so close — you understand. I had said farewell to happiness. I thought one might live usefully without it. Many have to. I found that I had to pay extravagantly for any that came my way.''

'I can't remember what happened then. We were interrupted, and I am sure that I never dwelt on the incident. Ever since Lewes died there were these hysterical outbursts; from the time She started to read Dante with me they began to subside. I gave all the credit to the prince of poets; I might have allowed myself some. I couldn't believe that such an average specimen of manhood could possibly mean anything to George Eliot. By the way, I was going through old papers the other day and I found some copies of my sister Zibbie's letters to my mother at the height of the Anna Jay crisis. It hasn't anything to do with our main task, but I thought they might interest you. You will get an idea of how our family operated. I had quite forgotten about them. They are in my study on my desk. I put your name on the envelope. I meant to hand it over on Sunday. Don't lose them, like a good fellow. They may be of interest some day to some of the family.'

With the grim assistance of Mrs P. who, I could see, took a jaundiced view of anyone taking anything away, I left armed with the large envelope of letters.

I went through them after supper; they were all from Zibbie, as the Crosses called the eldest sister Elizabeth, and except the first they were written to Mrs Cross. I was interested to read the description of George Eliot receiving Zibbie, her first contact with the Cross family. Lewes had set up the meeting when he met them in Weybridge on a walking tour with Herbert Spencer. Mrs Cross knew Spencer of old, and threw an impromptu party. Lewes enjoyed his evening, and encouraged Zibbie to send her recently published poems to George Eliot. A year later the families met in Rome; before the year was out Zibbie was dead in child-bed.

In between she had taken an active interest in brother Johnnie's romances — he was in America — first with Miss Hoyt, then Miss Jay. I spent the evening taking notes. Next day, as I knew I was going to do a certain amount of sitting about waiting for people, I took the envelope with me, leaving my notes at home. Nothing so far had let me see how Johnnie appeared to his family, of whom only Jim was new to me. I assumed that he was the brother who stayed in America and married — twice.

After supper I intended to return to work on the letters, but the envelope was nowhere to be seen. Then I remembered the crowded bus I had jumped on to in Fleet Street and a man saying 'I think you've dropped something, chum' and picking up my *Times* (I had been reading it at the bus stop). I must have dropped the envelope then or, perhaps, I left it in one of the newspaper offices I had been visiting. How would I face Johnnie? This was the sort of incident which would undermine all his confidence. I spent the best part of the next day trying to retrace my foot-steps, and I called at the lost property office. Nothing. What was my best course? Should I take Mrs P. into my confidence? Or write and confess and ask to be forgiven? Or wait until after Sunday's outing? Otherwise the day would be ruined for both of us. I should never know what happened in Venice. Finally, I decided to see how Sunday went and bide my time. I would have given a great deal not to have let him down like this. What an absent-minded ass I am.

Miserable, I looked at the notes I had taken. Even to myself they were well nigh incomprehensible, but at least I could put them into some shape and order. Johnnie, no doubt, could recall his American adventures, but these letters gave a touch of variety to Johnnie's sometimes laboured narrative.

I had copied out in full Zibbie's letter to a Scottish cousin after she had made the famous call on George Eliot (to whom, on Lewes's advice, she had sent her poems). It was 4th February 1868. Zibbie had come with her brother James, the one who married and settled in America — Zibbie's favourite.

'I was taken into G.E.'s kind heart on Sunday. I had much ado to keep from crying, her congratulations on that poor little book were so warm and touching — she put her hands into my muff and gave both my hands a strong embrace unseen by her husband or my brother — she said wonderful sweet things to me, but there was a great music in my ears and I did not very well hear them, but Jamie did. I liked the hour when we four sat round the fire and she made me warm my wretched feet and said she would take them under her special protection and her great face and her sacred eyes lighted up with laughter. We had such fun! Hers is the kindest fun. The vast price she must have paid to arrive at such perfection made me shudder.'

The other letters were principally about Johnnie's involvement with American girls, first Miss Hoyt, then Anna Jay. In matters of the heart Zibbie found her brother inept. He was accepted as the family financial adviser ('We must have a thorough consultation with Johnnie about it').

Zibbie had recently married Henry Bullock and they were living abroad, moving from northern Italy to Lucerne and Baden, waiting for a legacy from an aunt of Henry's to keep them afloat until Henry's uncle, the Admiral, died and he came into his splendid inheritance (Zibbie would be dead by then). Meanwhile she acts as family consultant in chief. ('Henry thinks that perhaps you have had enough Shakespeare.' Mrs Cross must have been worrying about her 'Monday Evenings'.) There was to be a ball in June. Zibbie is sent the list of names for suggestions. She is glad that 'Fod', the youngest sister, was told the facts of life before Anna Druce had her baby. ('My darling Mother, Ah, I wonder if I shall be so blest as to be doing the same work with you in four months from hence.')

But for my purposes what mattered were the references to Anna Jay. I tried to piece my rough notes together.

Before Miss Jay there had been a Miss Hoyt, but she was not well thought-of by the family. 'Your description of Anna Jay is most charming,' Zibbie writes in June, and two months later, I found this:

11th August 1868. 'It was a certain relief to me to see from my dear Jim's letter that it will probably be Anna Jay whom I figure to myself a good and innocent and artless young girl, and a lady. I had an instinctive fear of Miss Hoyt — but surely he will be well-guided in this all-important matter. He has been all his life so unselfishly and tenderly devoted to others — and Jim knows pretty well whom he could love.'

A few months later Johnnie is planning to escape from the Jays by coming to England. But they came too. 'Get Johnnie quickly out of England,' Zibbie wrote. 'Johnnie and Nellie should spend May with us in Switzerland.' The Jays were not to be shaken off; they decided to come to Europe. In February 1869 Zibbie protests, 'He has had years of the Jays and may have years more of them and he had only a few months with us. Real rest and freedom of spirit strengthen him for work and for fighting afterwards — time is what he wants and if *she* is anything (which I doubt) what she wants.' The Jays had spoken of a 'family meeting'. 'This is all, as the General would say, *damned nonsense*. The families have nothing to do with it, which it would be well if her mother had recognized earlier. He can drop down on them in Lucerne or Zurich or Geneva if *he must* let the house. We think Johnnie should put off his English and Scotch visits.'

Plainly Zibbie thought her brother lacking in backbone where the Jays were concerned. They must have been friends of long standing. I had made this extract from another letter and, characteristically, didn't note the date.

'I am utterly discontented with Johnnie's proceedings and I long to get him away from mischief and danger. It will be a heavy misfortune if he drifts into the most serious decision of his life — he has not seen the right woman yet, and it is utter nonsense to talk of having lived his life, his love is yet to come, and it should be a blessed love and marriage indeed, if he gets what he deserves, but these women are not up to the mark and it will be very wrong of him when he *knows* better, when he has "such a mother'' that faith in womanhood beats in his blood, if he declines to a lower level than his true love.'

Did Mrs Cross pass on Zibbie's instructions for his campaign? Or send them as if from herself? Perhaps he would tell me, if the mess I had made of this matter didn't end our friendship. I should like to hear from him what prompted Zibbie's remark: 'Are the Jays still in London? I am very glad Johnnie is taking such a decided line with Mrs Jay.' Mrs Cross gets a letter of which I kept only this: 'Let the house. Johnnie must get away from *Weybridge* as soon as you can leave Anna [Druce] — he will thus get time to know his own mind.'

Some compromise was reached. Johnnie seems to have suggested a four-year moratorium after which the engagement could be renewed if both parties felt so inclined — a rather desperate expedient. Zibbie was anxious about it.

> 17th June 1869. 'My darling Mother, Until Mrs Jay has consented to a four years' farewell, I don't feel as if things were settled or that he is quite a free man. Very, very thankful that he has freed himself from a false position. Of course he ought to be married. Papa's wisdom: no-one should get married till he can't help it. Johnnie wants above all things a companion in a wife, and ten years is a great gulf between them. He has *lived* and she is a child incapable of sharing a single thought of his. I wonder at your regretting Miss H [oyt] for a moment. Some sweet bond some day if he will only have faith.'

And she was still doubtful when she wrote: 'I wonder at your regretting Miss Hoyt for a moment. She has married the only man she ought to have married and Johnnie must not marry until he feels as strongly as that man did — if he does not wait then there is much to lose (as he must have felt lately) and uncommonly little to gain, except trouble and a variety of miseries — but this is all *entre nous* unless he is a free man now.'

Reassurance came. Zibbie was free to mind her own business.

The Jays had packed it in. 'Oh well I know how profoundly thankful he will feel for his freedom, though you must be prepared for a reaction of desire for some sweet bond which some day will certainly be his.'

Johnnie went away with Mother and Eleanor, who had been ill. This was the time when Zibbie brought George Eliot and Johnnie together, when, goggle-eyed, he listened to her talking to his mother in the Minerva Hotel in Rome. They met again in the autumn at Weybridge when gloom, past and impending, brought the two families so close. Was Johnnie ever to look at another girl again? Or did his return to England mean a retreat from the New York marriage market and a vote at twenty-nine for life with Mother? He had not fallen in love with George Eliot. That would have suited a magazine story. Johnnie's amorous inclinations, from the evidence available, never burned with a hard, gem-like flame.

I would take my time and draw him out little by little — I wanted more background to the Jay story. Just as he had been avoiding coming clean about his honeymoon, so would I avoid as long as possible a showdown about the lost letters.

V

Johnnie

MRS P. IS highly suspicious of Colin. Nothing will convince her that he isn't the young man who stole my silver-handled umbrella when he came here on the look-out for first editions. I keep telling her not, but the woman won't listen. I can't have her insulting my guests; if she makes any references to umbrellas in Colin's hearing I'll put her in her place. 'He must have quite a fine collection by now if he takes one from every house he visits, but I suppose they have got wise to him now.' *That* after I had carefully explained to her that she was talking about a youth called Evans, who is Welsh, incidentally. She did see through the journalist chap with a name like a disease — what was it? Pox, or something of that nature — before I did. But Colin is not that sort of person. Damn it all, he is a member of my club. I made a mistake, though, in letting her know that I had been lunching with him the day I arrived home late on account of the fog. It wasn't his fault that the taxi ran into such a pea-souper on the way home. One doesn't expect them so early in autumn. What *did* it matter if I was an hour late for tea? We had plenty of time for our game of draughts after dinner. It's the only form of exercise she takes. Roars with laughter when I say that to her. She is not a bad sort, but I wish she would get over this mania about people stealing things. When that journalist fellow was here, she winked at me every time she came into the room as much as to say I shouldn't leave him alone with the silver. The trouble with women of her class is that from reading nothing except the *News of the World* they get a lurid view of life. I can never understand how a woman so ostentatiously respectable as Mrs P. can read a rag like that. It doesn't seem to shock her in the least. Of course, I wouldn't discuss it with her. She leaves it lying about, and I take a peep occasionally. Curiosity gets the better of me. It's strange how lax one becomes. I usedn't be able to take sweet things. Can't keep away from them nowadays. What a face the nieces pulled the other day when she said, 'Eat them up, sir,' when I was trying to hold back from the cherries in brandy they brought me. They know I like them. Did they think she said 'love' instead of 'sir'? I must confess I got that impression myself. If they believe we talk like that when we are on our own, they will make my life a misery until I agree to get rid of her. And that's the last thing I want to do.

She saw Anna out, and I am relying on her to see me out. She made us very comfortable at Sevenoaks. Never regretted letting the Tonbridge house stand idle. I was far better off with Anna, and she liked to have me there after Albert died and the children had left the nest. I always had the other to fall back on. Only a bachelor could afford such extravagance. *Bachelor*. What made me say that? Often when I wake up I'm blessed if I can remember where I am or what day of the month or year it is, but I never forget that I married George Eliot. Always think of her as 'George Eliot'. Strange. I suppose one of those trick-cyclists we are hearing so much about would have an explanation. To my discredit, no doubt. It may have been quite simply that having been on aunt and nephew terms for so long it was difficult to adjust to man-and-wife names. I was always 'Mr Cross' in letters to her friends, even after we got married. Before that I used to call her 'Beatrice', a trick I fell into during our Dante readings — She encouraged that sort of thing. She couldn't by any stretch of the imagination have called me 'Dante', but that 'Best beloved' shook me. No-one had ever called me anything like that before. And She was so formal and cautious as a rule.

Have to get up. Dammit. Just when I was comfortably settled. I won't have it in the room. Go to a nursing home before I'll let that happen. What we expected maids to put up with in the old days. As if they were a different creation. Often did it out the window. Disastrous on one occasion. Funny, though. Never had any slops to collect in my room. I wonder what they thought I did. I must creep out. That woman will hear me. Steady the Buffs. That's better. Feel rather dizzy though. The breathing apparatus is better when I'm out of bed. I'm caught either way. If Mrs P. were to suspect anything, she'd be on to that doctor, and he'd be round. After that 'no visitors' most likely.

The chamber-pot reminds me — the morning I came into her room in Verona — I saw it quite distinctly, but pretended I hadn't, stared out of the window and gabbled some nonsense about all the balconies there were in this city. I was developing a mania about balconies. Never thought about them before, but in Italy on this trip there seemed to be balconies everywhere. I dreamed about them. Did She notice the pot herself afterwards and wonder if I had? It may not have bothered her. She was plain-spoken about such matters, despising euphemism; this was partly her country upbringing (reared on a farm), partly from living with Lewes. He went in for being scientific. Shall I ever forget the time he told me that he looked in her water for blood? He may have, but why had he to tell me about it? Always inclined to repeat jokes in doubtful taste. She never seemed to mind.

What upset her, She used to say, was frivolous treatment of serious themes. She told me She walked out of a French theatre because love was being treated as a subject for farce. Dragged Lewes out too. He might have been enjoying himself. Lewes was always very nice to me and grateful for any help I was able to give them with her investments. But, even so, what a position for a man to get himself into! He had no money, earned very little and to have to ask the woman you are living with (whom the law won't let you marry) to help with the upkeep of your wife and her children is something I wouldn't like to have to do. Some of the children were Thornton Hunt's, but Lewes never seemed to mind that. He was wonderfully easy-going where domestic morals were concerned. A rum lot. Funny to think of a Cross in that *galère*. What would the Pater have thought of it all? I always suspected Lewes got a certain satisfaction from our being so utterly respectable, and he liked the Bullock Hall connection and the house parties at Six Mile Bottom, Turgenev and all that. How miserable I was with old Turgenev when we went on a shoot together. He was frankly past it, and I hadn't got over Mia Donna's death. We killed a few birds, and he snubbed me when I tried to engage him in book talk — 'You have never written a book, or you would not have asked that question.' And She liked the sort of family we were. They had bohemian and radical friends in plenty — all that homespun Coventry lot.

The wedding list — all her stage-management — with no-one invited but Crosses or Cross in-laws. I was forgetting Charles, decent, grateful, dim old Charles, longing to become a somebody in his own right. How funny he was about Anny Thackeray when he tramped round to her house to break the news. Her eyes were out on sticks, he said, as she drank in every word. I can see her. When he came to the statutory piece about G.E.'s 'influence', hoping it wouldn't be diminished, etc., Anny jumped down his throat. It would be, *of course*, but that wasn't what mattered, what mattered was doing what She wanted to do — marrying me — and telling the world to go to Hell. She was a brave woman, Anny said, and she admired her for it.

I wonder if I'll remember all this when Colin comes tomorrow. Must start to scribble things down when I think of them. I'd do it this minute if I could put my hand on my fountain-pen without having to get out of bed. If Mrs P. would only for once have minded her own business instead of carrying my clothes into the dressing-room last night, I could have reached out for it on the chair beside me; the pen was in the waistcoat pocket. Whatever I do I mustn't go wandering off at tangents when I am talking to Colin. I notice something peculiar about myself lately: when I try to recollect what happened in those few weeks between the time when we began to read together and when we decided on a day for our wedding, I can't get my mind to concentrate; like a dog set down in familiar territory, it goes flying off in all directions, following this trail and that. I suppose dogs know what they are looking for. I had no idea.

How flattered I was when She offered to read Dante with me. Who would not have been? Until then — since the funeral — my only excuse for calling was to discuss business. Now we had a project in common. It was quite impossible to keep up with her. She knew the three books backwards. But She was merciful. We never went on for too long. Why would this genius of a woman with so much on her mind bother herself to do this? I put it down to sheer benevolence, knowing She was well supplied with this commodity, but She seemed to look forward to our sessions, and I could not help but notice that at times when her health was being anxiously inquired after by callers, and friends were being turned away at the door, She never suggested interrupting our programme. I asked Willie for his opinion. He is the most detached of my siblings. I was astonished when he said 'There are some women who can't exist without a man just as there are men — neither of us is like that, thank God — who can't exist without a woman.'

At first I was offended. But I recovered myself. Willie at the best of times is unpredictable. At Venice, when She told the doctors there was madness in our family, was She thinking of Willie? She had laughed very heartily at my account of the time our house in Weybridge went on fire. Willie was told he had time to go in and rescue some valuables; in he went and came out with his toothbrush. That was what Diogenes would have done, was her comment. But it did not suggest that he was the man to advise me in my present crisis. We had a different set of values.

I went to her in answer to her letter of despair to discover that she had requests for money from a nephew of Lewes and from Madame Belloc, who was looking for £500. I had expected to hear something less mundane and I offered at once to take over her finances, be her bailiff; She could send her beggars to me in future. She thanked me with more fervour than my offer deserved — I was, after all, already in charge of her investments. 'Only one's husband can be delegated such difficult duties,' She said. 'I don't mind in the least, taking them on,' I said. She seemed to be overcome, kissed my two hands and asked me to leave her to consider. She was 'overwhelmed', She said. I put down her behaviour at the time to her extreme and prolonged depression. She was over-grateful for a small act of kindness. Lewes, after all, was not her husband nor a man of business, as I was, and She had delegated matters of this kind to him. When he was there these people would not have asked for money. It was not until I was writing the book that I saw a curious inconsistency in the letter itself. What brought me flying to her side was the first paragraph: *Dearest N. I am in dreadful need of your counsel. Pray come to me when you can — morning, afternoon, or evening. I shall dismiss anyone else.*

I put that in, of course, but the tone of the second paragraph clashed with the other so I left it out. It sounded so querulous. She complained that when She wrote to me at my office, I was at my club; when She addressed me at my club, I was at home; and when She looked for me at home, I had gone abroad on a visit.

The note of heartbreak was not there. I had hardly glanced at it, most probably, reading in it only a slight reproach. After forty-five years the truth dawned on me. My eagerness had been misinterpreted. My offer was one of the three proposals I had made to her unwittingly. I wasn't thinking of marriage. That I can swear. It would have seemed the height of impertinence. Her idyll with Lewes had left her shattered. Her heart had been buried in Highgate. I was her 'nephew Johnnie', young enough to be her son. Edith Simcox suspected something. Knew it from the way she tagged on to me that time I found her hanging about the porch when I called to enquire after the funeral. They used to tease me about Edith. 'You ought to marry her,' Lewes would say and then burst out laughing. She used to haunt them. We made a regular game of it, but I always sat her out. She was calling every day after Lewes died, madly anxious to know who was being let in. She went all the way to Weybridge to ask my sister Eleanor if I had been.

When I came that day the curtains were drawn and the shutters up on the windows of what used to be his study, where She had shut herself in. I could see from the way the maid looked at Edith that they were plagued with her visits, but when I saw what a miserable little picture she made in the light and the hungry look in her eyes — dogs look like that when you shut them out — I was sorry and sent in love from both of us. She had taken the air today and was the better of it, the maid informed us.

For the life of me, I couldn't shake Edith off after that. I waited to hear that she was going in the other direction before I said I was walking across the Park. It would not be out of her way she assured me, as if I had asked for her company. She never drew breath. Mrs Dowling, the cook, was given to gossiping and the neighbours were asking Edith about G.E.'s hysterical fits. She had dropped a hint to Brett to advise the staff not to gossip. Did I approve? Then she said something to the effect that it was a pity Charles 'wasn't up to it. You were the son She should have had, etc. They thought the world of you.' I discouraged her. I tried to talk her out of her gloom. When she said she was worried on G.E.'s account, shut up like that in the room with his papers — She might lose her reason — I refused to join in this jeremiad. Most natural, I assured her, so soon after a death. She had the spirit to pull herself out of it. I wasn't in the least alarmed. Edith changed her tack then and asked me when I saw her — 'You will be the first' — to tell her that if She would agree to see her, Edith promised faithfully she would not ask to be kissed.

'I couldn't possibly deliver such a message.' (We were standing at the lakeside. She looked like some species of waterfowl.) Her eyes were imploring me. I was slightly disgusted and wished to Heaven I had shaken her off at the outset.

'I didn't know Mr Lewes was so ill. He was lying on the sofa when I was shown in and he kissed me as he always did — me and Elma Stuart and no-one else. Did you ever notice? — I told him that I wanted to kiss her feet like Catholics kiss the feet on the Crucifix. Did he mind? Did I have his permission? He said he quite understood my feelings and I could kiss away so far as he was concerned as much as I wanted to or, rather, as much as *She* wanted me to. But She didn't understand the impulse. He did. Then She came in and when She sat down I threw myself on the hearthrug and kissed her feet, first taking her shoes off. ("No. No. Please not.") I don't think She minded really, and he was in the room. I never objected to his being there. Rather liked it, a witness of my devotion to our Madonna. I was never in the least jealous of him. Or of you. I want her to be worshipped. It's only that I think She gets taken in. I don't understand how Elma, for instance, can talk about her craft-work and clothes when I go to see her if she really cares as she says. The trouble over the kissing began when I kissed the hearthrug after She stood on it. She wrote to me that time, telling me not to do that again.'

We were near the Park gate. How glad I was to see a hansom. I took off in pursuit without as much as raising my hat.

But would Colin be interested in Edith? I think he ought to be. Without knowing about these intensities with women you can't hope to understand George Eliot. She regarded herself as their champion, saw herself as carrying some solemn responsibility. But only as a writer. That 'influence' of hers. Edith was up to her neck in women's politics, ran a shirt factory on enlightened principles with proper wages — a move against the sweat shops. I got my shirts from her. 'Better look out or she will poison them one of these days,' Lewes said. All by the way of joke, of course.

What will Colin make of these women? When I was writing the book I was an innocent. I thought that sapphist deviations had vanished with the Greeks. I couldn't reconcile that sort of thing with my attitude to women. Colin is up-to-date. He will not accept that. I see trouble ahead. Not that I could ever be persuaded that unnatural behaviour was ever a temptation to her, but there was no denying the extraordinary effect She had on some members of her own sex. Edith spent her time after my dear one's death making up to anyone who knew her. She called on me regularly and on my sisters, with whom she had nothing in common.

Maria Congreve was one of the women Charles was sent to see. Whatever happened at the interview, Charles could never be persuaded to give a full account of it, and Maria took three weeks to answer George Eliot's letter, breaking the news. As a Positivist she believed in perpetual widowhood; but that wasn't what upset her so much. Edith told me long after that Maria had confided in her that she 'loved my darling lover-wise'. I tried to shut her up — Anna was in the room — but that Edith Simcox woman was shameless. She seemed to take a perverse pleasure in repeating Maria's confidence. Once, apparently, George Eliot and she met after a lapse of months; Maria's heart was palpitating so violently that to avoid breaking down she forced herself into a calm and seemed cold; whereupon G.E. rushed out of the room in tears. Lewes was there. He signed to Maria not to follow her, and with a breaking heart she sat out the call. What is Colin going to make of that? The odd part of it is how tolerant Lewes was. I don't think he had any principles where sexual morals were concerned. Nothing shocked him. He encouraged Edith. She told me about the last interview that she had with my dearest — who had frequently checked her expressions of devotion. G.E. was preparing her for the discovery of our marriage. She had already told her to stop referring to her as 'Mother', but this was to all intents a parting of ways. Edith has written it all in an autobiography which is somewhere in safe-keeping and will never see the light of day. She gave it to me word for word, hoping, silly creature, that I would use it in the biography. She was longing to go down in history as part of the George Eliot legend. I left her in no doubt about what I thought of that.

She was kissing George Eliot for all she was worth while 'her darling' (as she called her) assured her that the love of men and women for each other must always be better than any other, that it might shock her to hear that She had never cared very much for women; they had her sympathy but the friendship and intimacy of men was more to her. Edith said she had never doubted it and bade farewell with a lover's kiss, which she insisted on describing in detail. I think the little creature was quite as mad as her brother the clergyman who laughed so much at a sermon at Oxford that he fell out of the gallery.

That puts my darling in the clear, but if I bring up the subject will Colin be satisfied to treat it very circumspectly? If he doesn't I shall damn well exercise my veto. But if the news got about? Strachey! I pray God he never lays hands on that manuscript of

Edith's. What cruel fun he would make at my dearest one's expense.

The evening George Eliot told me about Chapman, not the whole story by any means — I had not seen her diary then — we were sitting on the sofa in her study. I had been reading her one of our favourite poems.

> The stars of midnight shall be dear
> To her; and she shall lean her ear
> In many a secret place
> Where rivulets dance their wayward round,
> And beauty born of murmuring sound
> Shall pass into her face.

When I had finished there was silence; then She said, 'How beautifully you read *lyric* verse.' I was flattered, and amused because it was so like her to qualify her praise, to make it strictly truthful. I passed the compliment off, but She protested. 'You mustn't undervalue yourself. You are quite an Apollo, you know.' Then She went on to tell me about the interview with Edith. I couldn't see its relevance. When She had finished, I asked, 'Do you expect more from men than from women?'

'No. I am thinking only of the homeliest things.'

'Such as?'

'A cuddle, for instance.'

'A . . . what did you say?'

'A cuddle, like the ones I used to get, and not over often, as a child.'

I looked so surprised that She burst out laughing. This was a change from our usual Dante and Beatrice note. I was aware of getting a glimpse into her life with Lewes. He used to cuddle her no doubt. Had I taken her literary allusions too seriously? I felt like a child, a solemn child, who doesn't know how grown-ups behave. My excuse: I was dealing with a genius. I knew nothing about the species. She was so polysyllabic and solemn on paper and so intense about anything She discussed, I had taken my cue from her and conducted our friendship in the most elevated manner possible. It was She who began it all, She who set the reverent tone. Now I felt ridiculous. But She continued to smile. Then She stretched out her arms. 'Come here to me, knight of the rueful countenance.' The door opened, and Brett came in with a tray. I blessed her. Supper had interrupted us. When it was disposed of, I did nothing to revive the moment. At parting I kissed her hands, as usual.

That must have been quite soon before the wedding. I can't remember precisely. I was in a condition of pure funk all this time and trying not to think of what lay ahead because I knew if I did my nerve might crack. I had a breakdown after the Jay business — I wasn't made for close encounters with women. I don't seem to have the equipment to deal with them. As for my bride — a week in bed with influenza cut the time for preparations short; She was rushing round the fashionable shops buying bonnets and dresses in a state of considerable excitement. My sisters were called in as aides-de-camp on these expeditions. There was no repetition of the cuddling episode. I was ashamed of my clumsiness, but more alarmed than ashamed because I couldn't get out of my head a picture of George Henry Lewes and George Eliot, lying side by side on the great bed I knew the appearance of so well — he long-haired and pock-marked, She . . . At that point I used to bring a curtain down, but up it would go again, and the struggle recommence. Did I ever go through such hell as in those days? A condemned criminal knows at least that peace will follow his ordeal.

Can I tell Colin about it? I am longing to. Why? Why am I eaten up by this urge? And it gets worse as I get older. I'm sure, if I live long enough, I'll tell Mrs P. in a weak moment. I'd be ashamed afterwards, as if I had made a beast of myself, but when the confessional urge takes hold I'm woefully at its mercy. I can tell Colin and then make sure he doesn't put it in. He will wait until after I'm dead and spill the beans then. Even if he promised not to, how could I be sure he would keep his word? I can't expect him to be more jealous of my dear one's reputation than I have been. The responsibility is mine. I will watch myself, play for time — I have treated him decently over the money. I can give him more later on. I do love it so, someone to tell it all to — at last.

It was a case of Elizabeth Barrett, with me as a makeshift Browning. 'Italy, Italy,' She would say with rapture in her eyes. 'You are so tender with me,' She would murmur at other times. All the last days before our marriage there was something like awe in her manner towards me. When I disparaged myself, she remonstrated with me, 'You have such wonderful self-control. You are the essence of chivalry.' I was bewildered. I liked to go to bed at eleven, but She sat up reading with increasing enjoyment the later the hour, her voice getting deeper and stronger. Furtively I rubbed my eyes; sometimes I had to keep them open with my fingers while begging her to leave off before She exhausted herself.

In the train, after the wedding, She let fall that we were staying in the hotel in which She had stopped with Lewes. I was profuse in apologies . . . if She had mentioned it . . . even now it might be possible. She squeezed my hand reassuringly.

'There wasn't a jealous bone in his body.'

When the hotel porter showed us to our apartment I told him to put my luggage in the smaller bedroom. When supper was cleared away we took a stroll out of doors. This was followed by the evening read. I left the choice to her and She read *The Scholar Gypsy*, extracting all the witchery from that charming poem. 'Now,' She said 'it's your turn.' I chose *Dover Beach*. It seemed appropriate. I came to the close,

> Ah, love, let us be true
> To one another! for the world, which seems
> To lie before us like a land of dreams,
> So various, so beautiful, so new,
> Hath really neither joy, nor love, nor light,

Nor certitude, nor peace, nor help for pain;
And we are here as on a darkling plain
Swept with confused alarms of struggle and flight,
Where ignorant armies clash by night.

Her eyes were full of tears. I thought it more tactful to pretend not to see them. I put the book down and in a brisk voice said we must get a good night's sleep as we had a long journey before us. Then I rang for a maid to assist her. There followed a decisive moment. 'Sweet dreams,' I said, kissed her dear forehead, and went into the smaller room, shutting the door.

'My door is always open,' She said on our first night in Paris. In Milan, coming in as always in her night attire to wake me soon after cock crow, She held my head. 'When shall I wake up beside you? You have been very good, very patient, the apple of courtesy. You will have your reward very soon. Verona is Juliet's city. Were you thinking of that?'

In Verona, I say that my stomach is upset. She goes into medical details at once. She is an authority on every subject. In Verona, glancing through into her bedroom, I see the pot under her bed. Verona became a city of balconies. Ledges from which birds took off and flew free. Murray said in his *Guide* that there are more balconies in Verona than in any other city in the world. I believe him. When I tell Mia Donna that, She asks if he has personally counted all the balconies in the other Italian cities. Balconies and chamber-pots — that is the impression of Italy I shall take home with me, when my head should be full of Mantegna and this noble city with its purple roofs and great campanile nestling in a bend of the swiftly-flowing Adige and the thought that our dear Dante was often here musing on his hard lot. Dante is responsible for a great deal. Who would have imagined that the warm air of Italy would have wrought such a transformation in the Beatrice I knew in England?

Up with the lark, always on the go; looking at everything; it took all my powers of persuasion to get her to rest in the middle of these long days, which always ended with a few hours of reading aloud, regardless of the hour. And as with our marriage which She said I proposed three times, She spoke of its consummation as something for which I was yearning and planning. But my manner had not changed. I was attentive and affectionate and trying desperately to cover up my poor spirits and lack of appetite for our holiday. Why did I not have it out with her? Perhaps because it was too late. I had put us both in a false position. She knew the state of the case; only as a protection to her pride had She manufactured the idea that I was the unsatisfied one, She the willing sacrifice. In one respect only had I changed in manner towards her. Since we married I kissed her forehead when we said 'good-night', as I used to kiss Mother's. Before we were married I kissed her hands whenever I met her or took my leave, whoever happened to be there. It defined our relation. It was She who began kissing on the lips, adding words such as 'Soon, very soon, my patient one.'

I was by no means clear what happened in practice, how, I mean to say, one set about it. I knew from watching people playing games — speaking as one who is a pretty good all-rounder — that there is the world of difference between theory and actually making the shot. Suddenly being left alone like that with a girl. I had heard of men visiting a prostitute to get the low-down before they got married. I was going to ask Paget about something along those lines, but his austerity put the wind up me. He would have told me to ask God for guidance. You were intended, I presume, to be so carried away by the charms of the young woman that events looked after themselves, more or less. But what about the girl? Would a nice girl get carried away by anything like that? It was all very difficult. A strange business; I had given up bothering about it long since. It thrusts itself on one's attention as part of growing-up. Plenty of exercise was the best remedy. After a certain age the idea of sex was unseemly; I'd have expected G.E., of all women, to have agreed with me about that. The whole subject presents insoluble problems. To anyone who believes in the Creation it is hard to understand why God did not make some adjustment that would differentiate man from the beasts in the mechanical aspect. Even to have put it in another part of the anatomy would have been heartening. If what I was talking about could take place without us having to undress, what a lot of indignity would be avoided. Why go to such lengths over concealment in daytime and then cast it all off at night? But one doesn't have to. I was forgetting. Mercifully it all takes place under the blankets and in the dark. One could pretend it hadn't happened as when someone has the misfortune to break wind.

It would have been better for both of us if I had told her that I found myself averse to love-making. Instead I was making myself ill to avoid it. I couldn't disguise this from her indefinitely. Exasperated, She asked me if I was feeling unwell. Why was I in such low spirits? After these questionings I used to struggle to throw off my depression. The prospect of sea-bathing at the Lido when we got to Venice became my great object. That would do the trick. Lack of exercise was undermining me. I was used to taking more than other men of my age. True, we were running round churches and galleries, trotting from dawn till dusk, but that, exhausting as it proved, was not exercise in the sense that I was accustomed to it. I was raving. In Venice we had a suite of rooms on the first floor of the Europa Hotel. Across the canal, at an angle of forty-five degrees, was the lofty portico and the front dome of Santa Maria della Salute and, looking across the lagoon, San Giorgio and its campanile were framed in the window.

'Is this not Paradise?' She said, her eyes shining. The view was certainly magnificent. We were standing in the drawing-room. 'But see the prospect from here.' She took my hand and led me into the larger bedroom. I had been in it already, having followed the porters and exchanged mutual expressions of good-will while I felt in my purse for what was appropriate. She used to reprove me for over-tipping, never having quite accustomed herself to comparative affluence and what is expected of it.

'From the bed, look at what your eyes will see when they first open.' The same view, in fact, of San Giorgio that we had just been looking at, but I didn't say so. She took the edge of the rather gaudy coverlet in her fine fingers as if she were testing the material. Her hands were still exquisite. It pleased me to kiss them. When I looked up, I saw a tear.

'Was it a mistake to come to Venice? You had been so happy here. If you find the associations too poignant, you will tell me. I shall understand.'

I was amazed at my cunning. By interpreting her tears and reminding her that She used to come to Venice with Lewes I was pushing her back into mourning. It was my only chance. But how sad it all was. Had She not brought up this idea of consummation, we could have enjoyed ourselves hugely. To stay in Venice with George Eliot was unbelievable good fortune, more than I had ever dared to dream of since that first meeting in Rome when I watched her when She was enchanting Mother and longed to join in the conversation.

'He would understand,' She said, taking my hand and pressing it. 'He utterly despised jealousy, besides he was very very fond of you, dearest beloved. Look at what you have done to me in these weeks. Now it is your turn. Think of him, if you like, smiling down on us, as he would, great generous soul.'

'I have a balcony in my room,' I said. 'Come let me show you.'

My room had a small bed and the same view, of course. It was the measure of our unease that we kept on referring to the view as we went from room to room as if a new one could be seen from each. 'I am glad you have a balcony,' She said. 'But I want you to think of this as your dressing-room. The other bed would have been large enough for Hercules and Omphale. Think of Hercules, my dearest beloved. Think of his twelve labours. He had strangled serpents and cleaned out the Augean stables, but it was when he received the golden apples of the Hesperides, remember, that he took on a godlike immortality.'

I had been Jove and Apollo and Pan, and I should not have felt so exasperated as I did at the latest metamorphosis. It was on the border line of mockery (or so it seemed) and untactful in our circumstances. A flicker of anger passed across her face when I failed to respond. 'You look tired. Should you take a rest? We can go out in the gondola when the sun is sinking. I want to be at your side when you are watching it.'

Instead of welcoming the suggestion, I started to fuss about Mr Bunney — clutching the first straw to hand. I had promised Ruskin I would call on him. He was the agent for Ruskin's Venetian pamphlets. We must start to read them this very evening. I became passionate all of a sudden about Mr Bunney and the pamphlets. As if She was humouring a child She said, 'Yes, dear. You do that. Don't stay too long away. I shall be missing you, remember.'

'It shouldn't take me long. He lives on the Riva degli Schiavoni, only a few minutes' walk if the calle is not crowded. Don't fuss if I am not back at once. You know how it is when an exile sees a face from home. I am sure he will want to have news of Ruskin. I can't be boorish. So, if I am a little late, you mustn't worry. By the way, what shall I say if he proposes calling on us? I am sure he will want to pay you his respects.'

'I dread meeting English people when I am abroad. I always have. Mr Bunney won't have heard about our marriage. If you tell him that Mrs Cross is not feeling quite herself — which is always true if one were perfectly candid — I think you can effectively discourage him. Do not, on any account, let him know who Mrs Cross is. She is no-one other than Mr Cross's wife in Venice, and proud of the distinction.'

It was true, She had always avoided English acquaintances abroad in Lewes's time; then it was part of the strategy of her informal marriage, as at home She made a rule of never calling on people: it was her way of protecting herself against the possibility of slights. She had made enquiries before we took rooms in the Europa to ensure that Mrs Bronson was not in residence next door; that lady and her international house parties were what my dear one was intent on avoiding. For the same reason we were having our meals in our apartment. I had to smile when She crossed the lobby of the hotel; She could have been a soldier emerging from safe cover, braving enemy fire.

It was quite deserted when I came out by what I thought of as the back of the hotel, because we used our gondola all the time. But when I entered the calle which leads from the Accademia bridge to San Marco the tide of traffic was intense. The whole population of Venice seemed to be making the same journey. I felt like a schoolboy playing truant. With my lady I should have turned back at once. She would have fainted in the press. I was enlivened by it. That chattering stream of people had in such abundance the vitality of which I had been drained in these anxious weeks. I enjoyed rubbing shoulders with the crowd even though a protective hand never left the wallet that pressed against my chest. I took a wicked pleasure in staring up the narrow entries and the side canals, fascinated by their mysterious squalor, the scum and sea-weed marking high water; in one, a drowned cat. I stood on little bridges and waited for a gondola to appear. The signal for me to move on was when the gondolier spotted me, then 'Gondola, gondola, gondola' went up at once like a sea-bird's cry. I went across the Piazza and made my way to the waterfront, passing the Danieli where I had wanted us to stay; She objected that her identity would be more at risk in such a haunt of celebrities.

Mr Bunney's studio was at No 4160. I knew no more about him than that he was Ruskin's agent and painting a picture of San Marco that the great man had commissioned. The door was shut. There was nothing to indicate whether Mr Bunney occupied the whole house or only an apartment. I knocked loudly. After a delay, a woman opened the door. She had the air of one who has heard a knock that she knows is not for her and commits herself to no civilities in answering it.

'The Signor Bunney. Sto cercando.'

'You want to see the Signor Bunney?'

'Prego.' She eyed me with an indolent curiosity as if I were a street accident. 'Di sopra.'

I wanted to ask her if she worked for him, but didn't know how to say it. After those months slaving at Dante I couldn't ask the simplest question. It was the measure of the confusion in my mind. And something in the half-insolence of the girl's manner disconcerted me. She was slovenly, sluttish, nothing Ruskinian about her.

'May I go upstairs? Di sopra?'

'Scusi?'

'Signor Bunney. Sto cercando.' I started to make signs. I wanted to push past her. She did then what I had never seen a woman do before, ran her eye very slowly down my body as if she was measuring me for a suit. There was a cool impudence about her expression that tried my temper. I wonder what Ruskin would have thought of the scene. The *impasse* might have resolved itself, but a voice came from further up: 'Who is it?' followed by the appearance of a genial bearded face round the head of the stairway.

'Mr Bunney?'

'At your service. Come upstairs.'

I was glad to escape from the lady and was uncomfortably aware of her scrutiny of my back view. Mr Bunney led the way into a studio. A table was covered with Ruskin Venetian pamphlets.

'You must get a ready sale for these,' I said. There were drawings presumably by himself round the walls. I asked his permission to look at them. The encounter with the woman had disturbed me. I made some deliberately casual reference to her. He assured me that she was merely a girl who worked for their landlady. He was much disposed to talk, asked me if I knew Ruskin, and when I said that I met him occasionally, became very enthusiastic. I must come and see the picture he was painting for Ruskin. Where was I staying? Was Mrs Cross with me? He would be delighted to be of service. Mrs Bunney would be enchanted to pay Mrs Cross her respects. I was in a quandary. She was so passionate about her incognito. The last person She wanted to meet was a compatriot anxious to make a fuss about her. But I saw that Mr Bunney had no idea who I was, and if I could be sure he did not know my wife's appearance there was no reason why I shouldn't introduce her as 'Mrs Cross' *tout court*. I left, carrying away booklets and a sketch of the Rialto Bridge, having engaged myself to come and see his huge St. Mark's picture where it was in store.

My dear one, how like a mother hen She fussed and fluttered when I came home weighted down with my purchases. I had to lie back in a chair and have eau de Cologne gently rubbed into my forehead. Why had I not used the gondola? It would have wafted me round San Marco in a trice. Instead I had rubbed shoulders with pickpockets in this overcrowded city. No-one travels on foot in Venice who can afford a gondola.

'Are you sure your money has not been taken? Stand up and let me see.' The business of searching me took longer than I relished, as if She were fumbling in a bran tub for a present. How I wished that She would not keep reminding me about my sex. Before I became a close friend of hers I didn't think about it for months at a time; but since our marriage, whenever we came close to one another, I felt as if I was expected to make some kind of demonstration. I pulled my wallet out to bring the proceedings to an end. She had not asked any questions about the visit.

But now She settled down at the table and in her thorough way looked at the Rialto drawing. This was one of the splendid things about her, the full consideration She gave to whatever one said to her or showed her. On the occasions when She thought She had fallen short, a long letter would follow to make up for her apparent inattention at the time. I remember my astonishment early in the 'nephew Johnnie' days when, after lunching at the Pines, I received a long explanation of her attitude towards conforming; She thought She had given me the wrong impression in our conversation at table. Inevitably this meant that Mr Bunney's conscientious effort was submitted to the same scrutiny as a Guardi would have been, and found lacking in the highest excellence.

'I paid only three guineas.'

That, She explained, was not the point. If the Christian message is true this is how we shall be judged on the Last Day. I saw at that moment why my darling, who can penetrate the human soul, is sometimes forbidding in her prose style. Handing down the Tables from the Mountain on her off-days, She makes one too conscious of their weight.

'What are we going to do about the Bunneys? He asked if Mrs Cross was travelling with me, which shows he hasn't a notion of who we are. I had to admit that She was, never realizing that this would involve us with a Mrs Bunney, who, I was assured, will be delighted to meet us. As a friend of Ruskin, his hero and patron, all his time is at our disposal. Bunney tells me that the Correr Museum is closed at the moment. I said we wanted to look again at the Carpaccio there since Ruskin declared it to be the best picture in the world. He smiled at that. "You know Mr Ruskin . . . *such* an enthusiast," but he has no doubt he will be able to prevail on the authority and gain admittance for any friends of Ruskin. That, you will have observed, is your claim to fame. If you wear a veil, I should think you will be able to maintain your alibi. I am chuckling to myself because, for once, I have an equal claim to fame with my wonderful wife.' We were happy at that moment, and even got round to discussing where the Bunney sketch would find a home — at Cheyne Walk or in her study at the Heights (we were keeping on the Witley retreat).

We were up before Venice was awake. When I heard her moving about, I leaped from my bed and called out that I was dressing when She came to the door. We had planned to go out before breakfast and walk along the Zattere to get the breeze from the Lagoon before the sun got up properly. There was no fear of meeting friends at that hour. She knew the city as if She had lived here all her life. I listened while She pointed out the shortcomings of San Giorgio, which I had formerly held in reverence.

Was it like this when She was with Lewes, I wondered? Did they take turns? When I came out with something of my own She listened with grave attention and perfect politeness and then, as gravely and as politely, showed me how I had managed somehow to miss the point or get it slightly wrong. This had a *very* tiring effect on the spirits.

Her erudition made our progress slow — we stopped before everything; She was familiar with everything; She knew what everyone had said about everything. When we got back to the hotel eventually, Mr Bunney was waiting for us, and joined us at breakfast. A nice enthusiastic little man; I was relieved when he failed to recognize George Eliot. He was triumphant; we could see the Carpaccio; he had arranged matters with the curator; it would be far pleasanter to have this private viewing instead of having to mingle with gaping tourists.

The picture is not one I would have expected Ruskin to like, two sluggish-looking women with protruding bosoms, staring vacantly into space. Their fair hair is frizzed-up, negro fashion, and, judging by the pair on display, they wore very high pattens, as if they walked on platforms (did they ever move?). An odd picture, certainly, rather over-crowded for my taste. Afterwards She told me the women were courtesans. For some reason, the little dogs in the picture convinced her of this, and the extreme slothfulness of the women's demeanour. I argued with her for once; the wife of a rich merchant led a most idle life in all probability. She over-rode me almost disdainfully. If further proof was necessary, one had only to look at the dogs. That and the fact that there were *two* women in the picture was conclusive. 'I don't understand why Mr Ruskin praised it so much. It looks to me like a fragment cut out of a larger picture.' I surrendered.

But She thanked Mr Bunney for having gone to so much trouble on our behalf, and She was her sweetest self to homely Mrs Bunney when we were taken to meet her and eat sugar cakes and drink tepid tea. The Carpaccio added to my state of depression. It was somehow disconcerting to find Mia Donna (as I called her in Venice) more knowing about courtesans than I was. It undermined my status as a man-of-the-world. Had She been offended by the subject I would have known perfectly how to soothe her outraged feelings.

But why should She have been? Had She not told me that Chaucer, Rabelais and Fielding were among authors She and Lewes used to read to each other for recreation? I dreaded more than ever the coming of night. Venice was the place of execution. I pleaded a sore thoat and concern for her health as a reason for postponing our first night together. Next night a finger cut in peeling an apple was expanded into a medical crisis during which I retired to recruit my strength. But I would run out of expedients in the course of a month. What made my lot worse were the awful dreams I was having. In one of them the slut at Bunney's house was sitting between the two whores in the Carpaccio painting. All three were looking into the street where I was staring up at them. The slut was peeling her blouse off provokingly and inviting me to compare the bosom she exposed thereby with the other women's. I felt unable to take my eyes away from the spectacle even when I was aware that someone was watching me. I hadn't the will power to detach myself. I heard my name. Her voice. She was on the balcony on the far side of the street. I turned to her then and pointed at the women as if to explain. She was not angry. She smiled. Then She beckoned to me. I was powerless to move. The dream became hopelessly confused at this point.

In my state of health her exalted tone was in itself enough to exhaust me. Even if there had not been the threat of consummation, it was always an effort to keep up with her emotionally and intellectually. She knew nothing of the jog-trot pace at which most of mankind was satisfied to travel. The effort to come up to her heights was killing me. How was I to tell her that?

She noticed that I ate nothing at supper, and was explaining my loss of appetite to me when I interrupted, 'I just feel rather unwell.'

A quick look of irritation was hardly perceptible. Her voice was all concern.

'You must see the doctor.'

'I am sure it will pass. I shall turn in after supper. I have been sleeping badly.'

'You know why?'

'Lack of exercise, most probably.'

'After locking your emotions up for so long you are frightened to release them. You are unable to measure their strength. You are like a man who has kept a tiger cub as a pet and has decided when it was fully grown to let it out of its cage. Dearest one, will you not let me show you that your tiger is a paper one, that there is nothing to be frightened of. In my arms you will have only sweet dreams. Together we will drive those hobgoblins of yours away. I feel proud that it was left to me to cure the pains of Anna Jay, to teach you that woman's love can heal as well as hurt. So long as you deny yourself the full expression of your unselfish love, you are putting yourself under an appalling strain. I have seen the result. I am worried. Let me look at you close. Johnnie, dearest Johnnie, your chivalry has made you ill.'

'I should keep you awake.'

'A risk that I will face cheerfully.'

'Not tonight. Really, I don't feel well enough. If I am not better by morning we can call a doctor then.' It had occurred to me that I might persuade the doctor to forbid any exertion on my part. I was reduced to such devices.

'Have it your own way.' Her face was expressionless. I slunk to bed.

I slept quite well and dressed as soon as I woke to anticipate her early morning call. I was feeling ashamed by then for even contemplating a conspiracy with an Italian doctor; it would be quite unworthy. When She came to call me I was already dressed and on the balcony taking in the good air blowing in from the Lagoon. She enquired after my health with a tragic face, but I was determined to keep off high drama, and assured her that I felt as fit as a fiddle. Instinct told me to keep the note light. In Greek tragedy I was lost and, as I said, the prospect outside was entrancing even though I felt less well than I pretended.

We walked this morning over the Rialto bridge, through the market which was beginning to get under weigh. These were the real Venetians, there were no tourists around except ourselves. As a result we became the target for every stall-holder. I was disconcerted, but my wonderful wife revelled in the scene. I remarked with what authority She examined the produce for sale. We bought grapes and strawberries and as we crossed the bridge I was warned against the laxative properties of the berries. We sat down under the shoulder of the bridge and drank coffee and were happy. I told her so: I wanted to add, 'What more do we want? Is this not perfection?' Before I could frame the sentence, she said, 'You deserve happiness. Venice will empty its cornucopia over your head. I seek no happiness for myself. I can only win it now by helping you to make up for lost time and a life lived for others.'

'Perhaps, in the end, we all live as we were meant to live. I have been more privileged than any man I know by having had such women to care for.'

The remark didn't please her. I always knew; she became excessively sweet when out of humour.

'The flies are bothering me. Shall we move on?'

But it was the merest breeze. We were on the best of terms by the time we came to the Ca Rezzonico where Browning's son lives in such splendour.

After lunch we were going to see one of my favourite churches, the Madonna del Orto, in our gondola. It is always a mistake to attempt to instruct her. She knew the church much better than I did, and liked in particular Tintoretto's painting of the BVM being presented in the temple. It is more human than most holy pictures; after a short while in Italy I long to look at ordinary people doing ordinary things in ordinary surroundings. She pointed out features that didn't please her which I hadn't noticed before. Half an hour was spent on the examination; my legs were beginning to give under me. I was longing to suggest we sat down, but She was on the move at once.

I had only remembered this one picture and always paid it a visit when I came to Venice with attendant Crosses in the past, but George Eliot remembered others (without resorting to Baedeker) and we were more than an hour in the church. How fluent She was, how much She knew: weak at the knees, I marvelled. I would have liked after that to have gone to Florian's, taken my ease, listened to the music, enjoyed their coffee and watched the world go by; but I knew this was out of bounds at this time of day; someone from England might see her. We had arranged to go next morning to the Accademia under Mr Bunney's guideship. Little did he know how superfluous his services were, but as he was so eager to help friends of his patron, it seemed ungrateful to refuse.

When our gondolier put us down at the hotel landing-place George Eliot went up to her room. I stayed behind to smoke a cigarette, I needed a respite until we met at luncheon and engaged again in an analysis of all we had seen that morning. This evening we were to watch the sunset on the lagoon and then come home to a special supper. I had made up my mind. However I had got myself into this situation, there was only one course open to me now. And then? It was not at all like being shot at dawn. Only one effort of will is required for that experience. But I couldn't think beyond this evening. If I did, panic would descend. I must drink as much as I could decently accommodate. In an alcoholic haze I might achieve the otherwise impossible. I finished my cigarette and went upstairs.

She had changed into an eastern robe, a most expensive-looking garment, making its first appearance. I thought at once of a priestess and arcane rites. It alarmed me, but I said that I admired it. She had bought it to please me. She blushed like a girl.

Lunching, which lasted for an hour, we discussed every picture we had seen. It was, as it were, the second time round, and I felt exhausted by the time we had disposed of our last Carpaccio.

'Now our siesta. My room is perfectly cool, come and stretch your long legs on the vast bed.'

'I promised Bunney I would call and arrange for our Accademia visit. If you take a rest now, I shall be back for tea and we might sit out on the balcony and read before we go out for our lagoon excursion.'

She had such respect for engagements that She didn't, as lesser mortals would have, attempt to persuade me to break mine, but gave a quick sigh and then, perfectly sweetly, asked to be remembered to Mr Bunney, and to Mrs Bunney, if I saw her. From that moment, until I left the apartment, we comported ourselves as if my getting out were a business requiring the most delicate negotiation.

I knew Bunney would account for a couple of hours. He loved to talk, but he was not at home and I had to arrange matters with his shy lady. Eleven o'clock next morning was arranged for our gallery visit.

On the way out I saw the slut. She smiled at me so provocatively that for a moment I hesitated; I was tempted to speak with her. Then I thought of Bunney upstairs and waved and went. But I could not go back to the hotel. I was in a state of intense restlessness. I turned back towards the Accademia bridge, leaving our hotel on my left and walked aimlessly through the back-ways, crossing at intervals narrow, fitfully-lighted canals. Venice of sinister possibilities. In a more tranquil mood I might have found it picturesque. 'Buona sera.' A woman in a dark entry. I turned back to see if she had spoken to me. A painted lady, rather stout. She had a small dog with her like one I had last seen in Carpaccio's painting of St. Augustine seeing a vision in his study. The lady had eyes like black buttons. How did I say to her: 'Teach me how to fornicate without desire. Teach me how to conquer physical aversion.' She understood. Without a word she turned a key in the door. I followed her, in silence, up a stairway less squalid than I would have expected from the meanness of the doorway. She signalled to me to stay where I was, then went on upstairs. I heard her say something and a man's growling answer. An argument was taking place, but I could not follow it. The male voice was complaining; she sounded plaintive. After a time there was more grumbling as whoever he was climbed yet another flight; the stairs creaking under his reluctant tread. After a slight delay her face appeared over the top of the staircase. She beckoned to me. On the next landing she was standing at an open door. Inside I could see a large brass bedstead. Her face was indistinct as she stepped to one side to let me pass through into a small shabby room with, here and there, pathetic attempts at boudoir fashion. On the bed the dog was busy scratching himself. I wondered was he to remain there during the performance.

I tried — God knows — to look the part. I even smiled at her, but it felt like a leer. Did she expect me to kiss her? Should I simply undress as if I were going to bathe? That seemed impolite. Would it do to shake hands? She was looking at me slyly; then, as if in answer to the unspoken questions, she grasped me suddenly by the genitals. I made an instinctive movement to protect myself. She nodded appraisingly as if she were a housewife sampling what was on offer at a butcher's stall.

'Quanto le devo?'

'Mille.'

'Grazie.'

'Prego.'

After each monosyllable we exchanged a bow. I pointed towards the bed. Never had I conducted any transaction with such a strict economy of language. She shook her head. I was completely at a loss. Then she said 'Mille' with a certain emphasis. I produced the money at once. Myself I would have thought it insulting to offer to pay, as it were, over the counter; but I supposed she had been cheated in the past. Delicacy was out of place here, but I would not have offended her deliberately. If she helped me I would be grateful. When I gave her twice what she asked she went off into a little firework display of gratitude. 'É molto carino. Grazie. Grazie. É molto gentile.' She became quite homely then, pointed to a hanger on the door for my coat, and began to undress. She was not wearing stays, and the whole operation, which I watched with a tightening sensation at the throat, lasted only as long as it took me to remove my shoes and stockings. I wished I knew some way of taking off one's trousers without looking furtive about it.

Undressed she was shapeless; her huge nipples like prunes and wiry black hair sprouting in all directions were hideous. Giving me the kindest grin imaginable, she bent down (not without further gross exposure), drew from under the bed a flowered chamber-pot, and plumped herself down on it, looking about her then with an expression of gentle meditation. Before she had completed the performance I had pulled on my stockings, pushed my feet into unlaced shoes, and was preparing to flee.

'Dove va?'

In answer I pulled another bundle of notes out of my purse and laid them on the bed.

'Cosa c'e?'

'Mi dispiace.'

Before she could say any more I opened the door and shut it behind me. I was downstairs in a few strides and did not look back. I only started to breathe again when I found myself among the slow-moving crowd. I saw a fellow-countryman — one knows them at a glance — staring at my feet. Only then did I realize that my shoes were unlaced. I put up my hand: my necktie was gone. Closer to home my reflection in a shop window told me I was without my hat. I decided to say I had let that fall into the water and confine replacements to the purchase of a necktie. I would be in a difficulty if She noticed it was not the one I was wearing when I went out.

As I crossed the hotel lobby I read in every eye perfect knowledge of my escapade; disapproval in some, disgust in others; in the large hall porter's, sly amusement. I walked naked before them across the interminable marble.

She was not in our living quarters when I came in; I slipped quietly into my dressing-room and changed into a silk robe I bought myself in Milan. It would match my wife's exotic gown. I didn't feel disgusted with myself, as I should have expected, relief rather at having come safely out of what might have been a nasty scrape. *Never again.* I sponged myself down with deliciously cold water and brushed and thoroughly combed out my hair and whiskers. Now I felt fit to meet her.

She was not on the balcony. Had I called out when I came into the apartment She would have come to greet me, but that I couldn't have done for fear She might have noticed the significant changes in my dress since I left her. Now I must wait until She appeared and say I had assumed She was asleep when I came in and trod carefully for fear of waking her. I could have knocked on her bedroom door, but I found that simple action beyond me. I felt shifty as I looked around me. The firmly shut door of her bedroom looked reproachful. I stared at its blank face and thought of all that had gone to the making of its message. In my review I saw my life as a series of surrenders, not to superior force, but to more urgent demands. Culture which, looked at from a distance, had such a soothing appearance, led me to this grim door. I imagined myself writing over it in letters of flame: ABANDON HOPE ALL YE WHO ENTER HERE.

I saw my imaginary graffito distinctly. I read it over, forming the words with my lips; then the letters blurred, faded, and gradually dissolved. There was no warning over the door when it opened — only as much as one opens a door to put the cat out. It had been firmly shut when I came in. I could swear to that. To remain like this, as if I were a burglar in the apartment, when we could have spoken to each other without raising our voices, was absurd. I was horribly self-conscious when I came closer to the door hoping She would be the first to speak. I was about to knock gently when my eyes met her reflection in a long mirror in the corner of the room — the room was full of mirrors. She was staring at herself and quite oblivious to my presence or to anything except the image in the glass which She was contemplating with absorbed distaste: the low forehead, grey eye, pendulous nose, huge mouth showing as She slowly opened it huge teeth, and that horse-like chin and jaw line. I dared not move. But, even if She had seen me, I was feeling nothing but tenderness for her at that moment. It was a moment, but it seemed to go on for ever, as if we were victims of Vesuvius, fated to stand in our Pompeian position until the end of time. Then, like a trained nurse stripping a bandage off a raw wound, She drew back her robe and stared at her naked self. The large face above made the white, shrivelled body look as if it belonged to somebody else — pathetic in its thinness, vulnerable in its nakedness; what little flesh there was clung loosely to the large-boned frame, from which the breasts like dry wrinkled figs hung low; there were deep creases across the flaccid stomach. I took it all in as I turned my eyes away and stepped back, but not quickly enough to escape a glimpse of a sad grey mat and thighs as thin as arms.

The robe dropped back into place when I knocked on the door. 'I wondered where you were, my dear,' I said. 'Mr Bunney sends his salutations. You have made a conquest there.' I might have run on for ever; the one catastrophe I knew I was incapable of coping with was silence. I assumed that our embarrassment was mutual, and already consigned by us both to the trunk of shared experience where it would lie unclaimed.

'Fetch me a drink of mineral water, Johnnie, if you please. It is in the ice box.'

Grateful, I turned away, altering my mirror-vision of her room. The side of the bed looked very close. From under it peeped a rose-patterned chamber-pot. Chamber-pots — balconies and chamber-pots — was that the picture of my honeymoon I would face the future with, who had lived in a water-colour world?

We did our best. I suggested a gondola ride before supper as far as Burano. We could watch the effects of sunset on the lagoon going out and the lights of Venice on the homeward journey. She agreed in a flurry of enthusiasm. We set out in silence, holding hands.

Our evening excursion: setting out in the gondola; used to her endless flow — everything that came under her eye provided a topic for instruction as a rule — I was not prepared for her silence. Newly wed, on our honeymoon in Venice, in a gondola on the lagoon as the sun was beginning to turn red — very soon the horizon would be aflame — we had only to clasp hands and look.

'Rose-red,' she whispered when we saw the light behind the Salute. I had started to say 'Blood-red,' and coughed to smother it.

The unusual silence of Mia Donna might have been supreme

content; lovers do not need words. But I couldn't deceive myself. Our lagoon trip which was to have been the overture to an operatic evening, culminating at our hotel in a Liebestod, was a grim charade. If we could have achieved cheerfulness by declaring ourselves, for the moment at least, emotionally bankrupt, I am sure we would have been well content. I know I should have been; what She had hoped for, I don't know even now, or what She ever saw in me except a good fellow, anxious to be of service. We were unhappy: I knew that.

In desperation I started to recite *A Toccata of Galuppi's*. The Venice setting, I suppose, putting it into my head. I know the poem by heart and when I gave a Browning reading at one of Mother's 'Mondays' it went down very well. I should, of course, have taken thought, but I plunged in at once as if I were striking up a tune on a guitar. I was desperate.

'Oh, Galuppi, Baldassaro . . .'

Suddenly I had acute misgivings; like a horse in the dark scenting danger ahead. But as in conversation, when fearful of having said the wrong thing, I rattled on desperately, out of control, like a car going downhill on one wheel.

'Here you come with your old music, and here's all the good it brings.'

Here I would have liked to pause and consider what boulders lay ahead. But to break off when I had begun in full voice was difficult, and as I was staring into her sad eyes, it would be more pointed to halt than to plunge on.

'Did young people take their pleasure when the sea was warm in May?'

As that line left my lips, I winced, and so did She. Did She know what lay ahead? Of course. She knew everything. The pain would soon be over if I hurried.

'Were you happy?' — 'Yes.' —

'And are you still as happy?' — 'Yes'.

'And you?'

I pressed her hand then: reassurance; there were tears at the back of her eyes.

'The soul, doubtless, is immortal — where a soul can be discerned.
Yours for instance: you know physics, something of geology,

Mathematics are your pastime . . .'

I wonder did the smile, asking for pity, that I gave her then look quite so fatuous as I felt? Two verses to go, and I would be free of my folly.

'As for Venice and her people, merely born to bloom and drop,
Here on earth they bore their fruitage, mirth and folly were the crop:
What of soul was left, I wonder, when the kissing had to stop?'

She put her hand very gently over my mouth. 'That will do for us to be getting on with,' She said in a whisper (not wanting the gondolier to hear).

For the rest of the journey we stared ahead, not pretending any more. Back at the hotel, I discovered a sore throat and complained about the smell under my window. I would report it to the management in the morning, bad enough to have to put up with it when the sun was out, but after dark . . . I may have sounded more excitable than I was aware of at the time, but my manner served my purpose. Tonight there were no hoverings; each went to his room after a swift kiss exchanged in flight in opposite directions. No reference was made to our appointment.

If we could have lain side by side that night how grateful I would have been. I had such dreams, they began, broke off, turned horrible. Sudden wakings — I was always drenched in sweat. Live and sleeping images merged so that I could not separate them. I seemed to be awake as I watched the girl at Bunney's place float into the balcony scene with Carpaccio's fat whores and become the other — the real one, the woman with the dog.

Whenever I tried to fix my thoughts on her there was a blank where her face should have been. When I was struggling in my dream to fix a mask on the blank, the whore turned her back on me: she was wearing my wife's eastern gown; she was staring at herself in the mirror; she turned her head and beckoned me to look; still she had no face. As I looked into the mirror she opened her gown. Now the image in the mirror had a face; but it was not the whore's face, and the wizened breasts and sagging flesh were . . . I woke up pulling at my eyes.

Being awake made very little difference; my real life and my dream life were often indistinguishable. I found it well-nigh impossible to give my attention later on in the morning to Mr Bunney when he was explaining to us the differences between his own painting of San Marco and the one we were gawking at by Gentile Bellini. I hadn't been able to find a word to say to his well-meaning wife. Some comment was called for. I should have left it to my dearest who would have said something memorable; instead I plunged in, and found myself talking about the balconies in Bellini's pictures and the Venetian chimney-pots which reminded me of . . . At this point, we were interrupted by a girl who had been copying a picture in the room. She came up to Mr Bunney and asked him to do her the honour of introducing her to George Eliot. Mr Bunney lost his head for a moment at the shock of discovering that he had been entertaining such an angel unawares.

George Eliot broke through the *impasse* by sweeping out of the room. I followed her. Outside She broke into tears which She tried valiantly to smother until we reached the hotel — a few minutes in our gondola. I heard her wailing in the bedroom behind the locked door, but what was I to do? My own crass behaviour was partly responsible for her breakdown, I knew. But She was always liable to fits of hysteria. She threw one at the first party She went to as a young woman, and on another occasion when Mother nearly set herself alight with a candle; and after Lewes died — God knows what went on at that house when She locked herself up with patient, grateful Charles and that household of women servants. I could only wait for the storm to blow itself out, as it did at last.

When the sounds of sobbing ceased I rang for luncheon to be brought up. I knocked gently on her door. She answered in her tragic voice, but I knew that She had recovered.

'Shall I bring you in your luncheon?' I asked.

'I should like a glass of wine.'

By the time I had poured this out She must have got out of bed and unlocked the door. It was ajar, and She was sitting in an easy chair.

'That is very kind.'

'You will be taking a siesta. You must not be tired this evening.'

I saw her face lighting up. I was saying what She wanted me to say.

'And you? My dearest one is not well. If you are not your old self by tomorrow, I shall insist on the doctor.'

Neither of us spoke about the catastrophe of the morning. We were feeling our way out of the maze into which we had led each other.

'Now I am going to undress. I shall not trouble the maid. Will you sit out on the balcony for quarter of an hour, then bring me back a report. I thought we might read more of Alfieri's biography before we go out again. It has been very good for your Italian. Do you agree?'

'Excellent.'

I went out on the balcony and looked across the canal at the front dome of the Salute. This view was one of the boasts of our hotel, and I was forever paying lip-service to it in phrases picked up from Ruskin. It compensated for the bad odour coming up from below, which I had learned to combat by keeping my handkerchief well-soaked in eau-de-Cologne. This afternoon I felt a dull disenchantment with Venice, including Santa Maria della Salute (She always spelled it out in full); the buttresses and too numerous figures round the dome looked to me like cake decorations, and I longed for the noble simplicity of St. Paul's and the prosaic familiarity of my London and the good sense of my countrymen (the gabble of the waiting gondoliers came up from right under where I sat). Italy was unsuitable for the English temperament: Browning's wife gave him a lot of trouble with her Italian enthusiasms, I had heard; Italy unhinged Ruskin's mind; it had had a miraculous effect on my dear one's health. It was killing me.

She was in bed when I looked in, sitting up in a lace coat, with a frilly cap of some kind on her head. My keen nostrils caught her favourite scent. She had laid it on with a heavy hand. I looked round for a chair. 'Come over here. Sit beside me. I don't shout across the room to my husband.' There was something in the emphasis She laid on 'husband' which made me dread what was coming.

'Nearer. There on the bed. I want to see you. I want to be able to touch you. What is making you unhappy? Ever since we came away you have assured me that you find the married state blissful. You are perfect in your courtesy, the most delightful companion a woman could have on a journey, but I would be deceiving myself if I hadn't noticed that something is eating at your heart. You weren't yourself today. If we can't do something to cure it you will become really ill. What is it? Remember we are man and wife, the closest bond that can exist between two living creatures. There should be no subject that affects us that we cannot discuss. I am so much older than you, and I have lived in close relations — the closest — with a man. It may be easier for both of us if I say the first word.'

'My dear, what is this all about?'

'The most sacred thing on earth. But first, I want to ask you a question. I trust it will not offend you, and I ask it only because if the answer is what I suspect we may able to banish your fears.'

'I have none. Please believe me. The Venice air may not suit me. I'll get used to it.'

She smiled as at a child. 'The clouds gathered long before we reached Venice. The trouble began when we made a certain appointment in Venice. Do you remember?'

The full horror broke on me.

'Every decent man is shy on his wedding night even if he has had previous experience. Will this be your first time? Tell your wife. She may be able to help you. I beg you not to feel inadequate; the idea might discourage some women, but I feel only gratitude that this so precious gift has been kept for me, a fly in amber that has not to be shared with anyone. No wonder, dearest love, you have been looking ill and acting strangely when you had this shy secret in your heart. This evening we will take the gondola as far as the Lido and come back across the lagoon when the city is full of points of light. You must order a feast for the gods to be waiting our return.'

I could say nothing. My heart was as heavy as lead. I wanted only to run away.

She had stopped talking. Her hands were playing with my coat collar. Wandering fingers felt between the lapels. I have a considerable growth of hair on my chest. It would have worried me if I were marrying a young woman, who might have found it distasteful. You never see it on statuary or in paintings; no hair except on the head. I had it everywhere else, but very little there. She curled my copious chest hair in her fingers, playing with it like a child with sea sand. I stiffened all over involuntarily.

'You are like a colt that is being broken in. I have often seen my father at the task. There was nothing in a farmer's line that he hadn't mastered. Lie perfectly still. Your Beatrice will show you there is nothing to fear.'

The vision in the long mirror leaped out at me. I had shut it out of my mind.

'Look at me. Read the message in my eyes. Forget all the pain. Leave yourself in the hands of your Beatrice.'

Her eyes were swimming in a sort of trance; the pupils staring, transfixed. I should kiss her now. She expected it. So close; her skin looked like a map drawn on parchment. I could have kissed her with loving reverence, but She did not wait for my kiss; her eyes closed, and as her head — huge it looked at that moment — moved from side to side in apparent ecstasy, I felt one of her long hands inside my shirt, hesitating, and then tentatively moving down. A spider's progress. I held my breath. My mouth was fixed in what felt like a horrid grimace. Had She kept silent I would have closed my eyes and pretended nothing was happening. We could trust each other to pretend. But She spoke. What the words were I can not remember; the humble sound of endearment was the last straw. I leaped out of bed, and then panicked. I have seen a dog rush as I did then from one room to another. In my own room the sunshine and the blue sky over the balcony mocked me. I came back into our sitting-room, into shadow, sat down on a chair, and began to shiver. I shivered until my bones rattled while my teeth were performing some mad dance of their own. I was frightened. But the attack subsided, and when it did I changed into night gear and crawled into bed. I was cold.

'Are you all right?' Her voice at the door.

Before answering I put my head deeper into the pillow and

pulled the bedclothes tighter round me.

'I got a sudden attack. Too much sun, I reckon. I will try to sleep it off. Would you be a dear and draw the curtains. The light hurts my eyes.'

'I'll send for the doctor.'

She pulled across the curtains and tucked me in motherwise. Sun-stroke was an inspiration; a magic formula; a face-saver. Neither of us would mention that only yesterday I had doubted that the sea was hot enough yet for sea-bathing. The doctor would get us out of our impasse.

The doctor, when he called, was very thorough. He prided himself, I could see, on his rather bad English. My countrymen are probably pretty stereotyped when they need a doctor in Venice. We went through the usual rigmarole. He looked astonished when I assured him that I had not suffered from bowel troubles, frowned, seeming to suggest that he had been sent for on false pretences. When I made a passing reference to the balcony — merely to change the conversation — he darted out to inspect and on his return asked if I had got a 'veery narstee' smell. 'The canal is always rather smelly; one gets used to it.' This he wouldn't have at all. The smell under my window was exceptional. It must be reported. I could see that he was greatly relieved to have come across a possible cause of my temperature and pulse. On no account was I to get up; he would write a prescription, and the hotel would send out someone to the chemist. Then, with a great many bows, he left me.

In the delirium of those hours that scene with the doctor stands out. Not only because there was something slightly ludicrous about it; I knew what was the matter with me, but no doctor could prescribe for it.

Voices in the next room; his shrill, hers vibrant. I caught the edge of hysteria on hers. She was saying that I did not get enough exercise. He was fighting for his 'veery narstee' smell explanation. (Did he suspect I might be developing typhoid fever? It took some time to appear, I had always understood. I had ceased to care.) Then I sat up, to hear better. She was telling the doctor that I had had breakdowns of this nature before; there was madness in the family. This riveted me. What possessed her? It was untrue; I had gone through a bad patch after the Anna Jay business certainly, but that was the usual distress in those situations. Willie was a funny chap in some ways, but sane by the most exacting standards. The girls were as sound as bells. The only delicate member of the family was a young brother, but he died as a child. Why was She inventing troubles? It was the normality of our family that had recommended us to her in the first instance. Surrounded as they were by theorists, She had often told me, Lewes and She found our cheerful common sense a tonic. But something in my recent behaviour must have given her the impression that my mind was disturbed. Did She *really* think I was mad, that She was married to a lunatic? On top of every other eerie experience I had encountered on this visit to Venice this was the snapping-place. It broke my resistance. One impulse was to go in and confront them; the other to get out and escape. There was only the balcony.

I sniffed. Yes. There was a bad smell. Not so bad as Billingsgate, but still — a bad smell. The voices of the gondoliers came up to me. I leaned out to see if I could recognize our gondolier. I couldn't see so far in and under. The water looked very close; a gleam of sunlight winked, then danced away. Another took its place. Green water with layer after layer of rainbow-patterned silk spread out across it, swaying gently, indolent, utterly restful. Peace. I fell into its arms. Cold, cold, dark, down, always going down, slower now; then light above me, far away. I reach towards it. Struggle. Choke for breath. Voices seem to come from a long distance. I ignore them. I want to keep this peace. The voices now are very close. They are coming to take it away.

'Va via! Lascia mi morire!' I cried.

Hands are pulling at me. A dark face stares into mine. I give in. Now shut eyes and behave like a corpse. I know exactly what happened, but I can never explain. No-one would understand. But I understand everything. With that immersion, leaps, fallings, balconies, chimney pots, chamber-pots, women's faces in dreams and mirrors — all fall into place with the beautiful simplicity for a mathematical solution. I had jumped free. Ever since I heard her telling the doctor that there was madness in my family my course of action became clear and imperative.

Now I was feeling like a naughty child. I would listen and not argue, do as I was told. Nothing would ever be quite the same again, but I had exorcised my demon. I felt so content; I could never explain. I had found a way to say what I had not been able to find words for. Meanwhile I was keeping my eyes closed and playing the corpse part. Soon the doctor arrived. He was in his element directing operations. The hotel manager's voice was plaintive. I found it hard not to smile. What was he going to tell the other guests? This was not the sort of thing that happened at the Hotel Europa. I was carried upstairs.

She shrieked. Then everyone began to talk at once.

While warm water and hot towels were being applied to me by servants, the doctor tried to soothe her. The manager hovered in the doorway, looking bewildered. It was a thoroughly embarrassing situation. Someone had to do something to break the deadlock. Like Lazarus I rose and went to her. She had thrown herself on to the bed with her face in the pillow which She pulled about and beat with clenched hands while She wailed disconsolately. Astonished faces were peering into the apartment, and guests were asking the manager what was the matter. He, poor fellow, was dancing a jig in his efforts to offer sympathy in the bedroom and offer explanations at the door. 'C'e stata una disgrazia.' 'Mia Donna. I am well again. Please stop crying.' At that She turned her head round and shot a baleful glance at me. Her eyes were glazed. But suspicion left her face when I put my arms gently round her. She did not stop crying at once, but now She was sobbing gently like a tired child. I concentrated on her while the manager and doctor gradually established order.

The word 'Gondolieri' was so much in the air that it sounded like a refrain. Yes, indeed, they would have to be rewarded (she sought them out next day, thanked each of them, and donated lavish sums — how much She never told me).

Now that the hysterical fit was over my wife showed her mettle. I was restored to bed and examined again by the doctor, who muttered 'febre'. Regular applications of ice packs to my head and a concoction he would have sent to me by the chemist was his treatment while he waited to see how the fever developed. He suggested a nurse, but She insisted that if any nursing was required it would be performed by no-one but her. Then came an eloquent interlude when a carpenter was sent in to fix locks to the windows of our balconies.

'I have sent a telegram to Willie,' She informed me.

I was feeling invalidish, nothing more drastic than that, and glad to hear Willie was coming — no-one better to defuse the situation. The balcony incident had fallen into place, an unmentionable symptom of a sudden fever. 'I don't see what is to be gained from referring to it,' She said. 'There is always a possibility of misunderstandings. Rumours get around. We don't want to give gobbets to the gossips. There is bound to be some talk. I hope Willie comes soon and you will be fit enough to travel. My idea is that we should take our time and go via Germany and the spas where George and I so often went in search of health.'

I agreed with everything: I felt fit to go at once, but it seemed unkind to say so. When She offered to read to me, I said I felt unable to concentrate quite so soon. Listening to her reading aloud in her splendid voice was too like going to matins. I longed for mundane occupation. It would be a relief to get home and start to superintend the move to Cheyne Walk. My admirable brother-in-law Albert Druce was busy, I knew, making sure our wishes were being realized — her little study was to be a writer's dream room. I longed to take over his duties as supervisor.

She hired a piano and played for hours on end — what a range She had! She made Bach and Beethoven speak for her. Sometimes She must have thought that She was betraying herself or, perhaps, indulging herself too much. Then She would come into my room and tell me to command her. She had decided long ago what music I liked best without having to put me to the question and took it as a sign that my fever had not yet gone down when I asked for a little Chopin. She was so sure that I would want Burns set to music or

Moore's melodies, which dear Zibbie used to sing so charmingly; her asking me was only graciousness.

Chopin's melancholy belonged to her. She said as much, played him for half an hour, then broke into some gypsy tantrum of Liszt's to relieve her feelings. Her manner towards me was subtly different from what it had ever been before. My health and family history, not her age, forbade any recurrence of our fiasco. I, not She, was the weaker vessel. The plunge into the canal rang down the curtain on act two. The mood for act three was gentle resignation and immense good will.

Sending for Willie was an inspiration; his phlegmatic personality exactly suited our situation. Ever since he had been shipwrecked in youth and survived the experience, he felt that the world had done its worst to him. He became the arch-deflationer, would have put his feet up to the Fire of London, and I like to tell him that he will be picked out on the Day of Judgement as the only person present smoking a cigar. To an indifferent spectator the situation was richly comical.

Here was I, the central figure in the drama, lying in bed, perfectly comfortable, with a doctor in regular attendance and another called in for consultation. Dr Richetti's problem — as She explained to me — was to reconcile the mildness of my symptoms with the gravity of my illness. Her knowledge of medicine (as of everything) was encyclopaedic, and She discussed my case with the doctors endlessly. The hotel management was also acutely concerned — the matter of the 'veery narstee' smell under my window had been raised and the staff was offering prayers for my recovery. I needed a rest, but I felt pleasantly convalescent and washed white as snow by my recent immersion. My worry was for her. She had taken on new life abroad, and it was pitiful to have made her so *distraite*. She had sent Willie two telegrams, he told me, and I noticed when I looked at her diary (later) that She had recorded his arrival on two consecutive evenings. She was beside herself.

His robust presence was certainly reassuring — an antidote to the highly-strung Italian medicos. Standing at my bedside, looking quizzical, he pronounced, 'I must say he seems all right to me.

What came over you, Johnnie, to give us all such a fright? You look a little under-the-weather yourself, sister-in-law.' I was delighted by this essence of Willie. He brought with him to that stuffy room the clean air of Surrey.

Have to get up again. Only ten o'clock. Dammit. I would have sworn I had been in bed for hours. What did Willie make of it all? I'd like to think about that, but I had better attend to what I am doing. Who would be old? Sight is the trouble; can't see properly; don't notice things. It isn't that one has become slack on purpose or need looking after like a baby. Dribbling on the bib and all that sort of thing. Mind off the job in hand at times. Bound to admit it. Awkward sometimes. Flies open in the club that day. Mrs P. never afraid to tell me. Nieces won't. Humiliating. Well, that's done. How inviting bed looks, you have only to get out of it for a second to realize how delicious it is.

Haven't thought about Willie for ages. He came up trumps that time, took over all our travel arrangements, dealt with porters, drivers, hotels, etc. in that unobtrusive way of his. Verona, Trent, Bozen, Innsbruck — rests on the flight. But we pitched camp at Innsbruck. She probably felt safe there, with Italy behind us. Our morning walks began again, and the evening readings. Willie kept at a tactful distance, getting himself involved in neither. Mia Donna was in Florence Nightingale mood. I was the invalided soldier. Willie was always there when wanted, but for the rest found his own amusements. I caught glimpses of him sitting at tables in the gardens, listening to the band, taking his ease outside inns, smoking cigars, a tankard before him. I envied him a little. I enjoyed the early morning walks (Willie was still in bed) but I could have dispensed with the resumption of our evening studies. She took over the reading aloud. 'Little extra calls on me' was how She described it in her letters home. I would have been more than content if She had confined us to novels, but She had persuaded herself that I shared her passion for philology. Looking back I can see that She may well have been chafing under lack of inspiration for a novel. That enormous intellect had to exercise itself and was unused to light diets. I accepted my role as a wounded soldier. It solved the great problem and kept us in countenance. We went to Wildbad where we took the baths. The spa is on the edge of the Black Forest, and we enjoyed long walks through the countryside with day trips to Baden. We praised the air. Nowadays people don't take so much notice of these things, but we were living in a smellier world and the fogs in London were appalling.

At Baden Willie left us. What a quizzical look he gave us when he came into our room to say 'good-bye'. I was lying back in my chair, She was grappling with a past participle. He might have been thinking of Mother's Monday evenings. What would she think if she saw her son now? Shakespeare is a bagatelle after a couple of hours of Sanskrit.

'I think your invalid is fully recovered. I can leave you with a good conscience.'

I watched her when Willie was excusing himself. As I had walked more than ten miles that day and we had been taking long carriage excursions, it was clear that I was out of the wood. The point She made was that he need not worry on *her* account. A call on her such as the present one She had always responded to. The threat lay in the future. 'It seems to me more natural to have anxiety than to be free from it. I only hope that I won't run down like a jellyfish now that it is over. I astonish myself by my freedom from ailments.'

'You must try not to regard them as inevitable.' Willie's very typical remark did not go down well.

'Dear Willie,' She said when he finally departed, 'always so liable to be out of tune on his top notes.'

VII

Colin

I HAVE HAD the most awful row with Laura. I hadn't realized that she had arranged a formal entertainment for Sunday evening. A family gathering and eminently missable was the impression I got, and I was quite unprepared for the *froideur* that greeted my begging-off for the occasion. I thought the largesse had converted my girl to the Johnnie Cross project — we are, after all, getting married on the strength of it (and before Johnnie came along the prospect was dim) but she has not changed her view that I am wasting time that could be put to better use, indulging an old man's senile mania for reminiscence. How long was it going to go on? When time ran out, would he pay for another instalment? I detected shades of disappointment in me under her coldness towards the enterprise. It all came out on the telephone, and when I stood my ground, she slammed down the receiver. I didn't call back. I couldn't if I were not prepared to hand in my gun. And I won't do that. Not now. Something tells me I must not let this opportunity slip. We have been making little forays down cul-de-sacs on my recent visits. I promised Mrs P. that I wouldn't excite him, but he left me in no doubt that Sunday is going to be a special occasion. He is getting out the last bottle of his best claret, a present from William Henry Bullock-Hall on his fiftieth birthday. Two dozen — he has been keeping the last for a great occasion. Nothing had come up to the imagined standard, but now, he told me, he was going to break a silence of forty-four years and tell me what happened in Venice. If I disappoint him when he has been so liberal of late, he may go off the whole project — he can be very touchy. I can't take the risk, and Laura's aunts and uncles and first and second cousins will have to whistle. I am a professional, after all. I can't fall down on the job for the sake of a dinner party.

'Can't the old man wait for two days? What else has he to do?'

'You don't understand. He is eighty-four, almost bed-ridden. He has nothing else to think about, and he has been planning this ceremony for days.'

'So have I, and put my mother to no end of bother. I don't know how I can break the news to her.'

'I can't let the old man down, Laura.'

'But you can let me down. Is that it? I should be grateful, I suppose, for the chance to mark my book. I can't rely on you.'

The arguing and nagging went on through three sets of warning pips, then rage, frustration and inbred dislike of extravagance came together; half-way through a sentence I realized that I was talking to a dead wire. It spoiled an evening and the day following, but I will confess that I woke up on Sunday feeling bobbish, looking forward to the day ahead. After all, it was something to hear from the lips of George Eliot's husband secrets he might have told to Henry James, and had not. Laura would come round.

'Come at twelve,' I had been told. Mrs P. would be at church but there was a housemaid to let me in. He would fuss if I were a minute late and get thrown off-balance if I arrived a moment too soon — his toilet took a great deal of the morning. He no longer kept a valet (some trouble with Mrs P., I gathered. He hadn't gone into it).

I gave myself plenty of time and arrived at Chester Square — at the church end — at eleven forty-five, stopped, lit a cigarette, and took the longest way round, walking slowly. I was carrying a bunch of chrysanthemums for Mrs P.

When the narrow road leading to Lower Belgrave Street came into view, I noticed something odd about the appearance of No 88. It looked like a black tooth in a row of white ones; the blinds were down. Death had come before me; now I would never have to confess that I had lost the letters.

VIII

Colin

It was Laura's idea that we should go to Venice for the honeymoon, her way of making up to me for the aborted book and that sad Sunday and her bad temper on the telephone. (As it turned out, the dinner-party had to be cancelled at the last moment. Laura's dad got one of his asthmatic attacks.)

We booked a room on the first floor of the Hotel Europa, with a balcony overlooking the canal. I was too grateful to my girl for this effort to empathize with my disappointment even to hint that she had got it wrong. The last thing I needed was to share a room with Johnnie Cross and George Eliot on *my* honeymoon; it required an effort to dispel the recurring image of 88 Chester Square on that miserable Sunday.

But the Cross episode had been an experience I would not have forgone, and I was very well aware that we owed our present bliss to that nice old man.

We were married in Edinburgh during a blizzard, took an express to London, spent the first night in Garland's Hotel (round the corner from the Ritz) and set off next morning on that long, luxurious train journey, interrupted while we rocked together on our narrow berth crossing that nasty ditch at Dover. We were as happy as Larry.

'I wonder whose room this was,' she said in Venice when the porter put down our bags and left us to ourselves at last.

'Let's not think of them tonight. I want to concentrate on us,' I said.

When I woke the next morning the room was full of light. I looked at the mop of hair beside me on the pillow; Laura was still asleep, her mouth slightly open, as if she were blowing out a match. Very gently, I slipped out of bed, and drew the curtains. I was looking at the dome of the Salute; beside it, where the mouth of the canal opened as it entered the lagoon, San Giorgio

Maggiore was staring at me across the water. Someone was sitting on the church steps. A man, I decided, and pretended that it was Johnnie Cross. In the circumstances, it seemed unfriendly not to wave. I had just spent my happiest night on earth at his expense. ('We should have waited until we had come here. It was what I had intended. On the other hand . . .')

Did he wave back? I fancied so; it was only a game; he couldn't have seen me. I wanted so much to thank him and say how sorry I was that he might have been feeling unhappy in this blessed room. With very little evidence I had made my mind up that this *was* his room, and I decided that he can't have been happy here when he was feeling so ill. What happened? What would he have told me at our Sunday lunch? If you concentrate on one person at another table in a restaurant you will pick out their voice after a while over the surrounding noise. If I concentrated very hard on that little figure in the distance, might he not get some sort of wireless message from me? And would he in return broadcast that lost message?

What were the facts: in May George Eliot went abroad in high spirits, full of new energy, and — marvellously for her — free of all physical complaints. She was never ill on her trip, but took to her bed soon after her return. She was dead before Christmas. Johnnie, on the other hand, was in wretched health and spirits before he came away, stayed that way when he came abroad, and collapsed with a bout of fever in Venice. After that he never looked back; he was quick in casting off the fever, quite fit when he came home and remained so — from what he told me — for the next forty-four years.

What happened in Venice? One explanation could have been that Johnnie, once he overcame his initial shyness, performed his husband's part with excessive enthusiasm and, in his state of health, overdid it. He succumbed to germs in Venice. He was comparatively a young man and an accomplished athlete who did anything he undertook conscientiously. However much he might have resisted the idea of going to bed with his wife it would have been difficult to refuse if She had kept nagging at him. Supposing he gave in, from sheer politeness, or for peace — suppose he did, and found he was good at it, and even liked it — having no comparison to make. He might have forgotten Sir James's cautions and worn out his bride and himself. She would have been enchanted; it was the one compliment that he had never paid her, and the one She wanted most. She may have thought of Anny Thackeray with *her* young husband as She gave Johnnie the right of way. Nature, eventually, would have asserted herself. Johnnie, run down to begin with, must have been an autumn leaf when they arrived in Venice. Quite soon he succumbed to the local germs (there was a bad drain under his window. It says so in Murray). As for her: an amorous husband had swollen her emotional capital, She had enough to live on until they got back to England. Until then She put her energies into nursing him. Long before they reached home, he was perfectly well. Whether or not they resumed their married life, the damage to her was already done. The euphoria that sustained her through his illness evaporated when he was well. Sir James, when he looked at them, must have shaken his head. Her familiar routine of autumn illnesses recommenced; every germ in London came to call. Her hospitality to the breed was notorious. The throat trouble which proved fatal was a haphazard blow; every part of her except that marvellous brain was worn out.

'Darling.'

Laura beside me. I put an arm round her shoulders. We look out together. Neither speaks at first.

'Who are you waving at?'

'Johnnie Cross. Can you see? He is sitting on the San Giorgio steps, all by himself. Wave at him. He wanted to meet you. Told me to bring you to lunch some day.'

Laura gave a perfunctory wave. 'I didn't tell you: I met someone in Edinburgh who knew about him. Did you know he was Scottish?'

'He told me. He was rather proud of it.'

'Sellar, the name of this person was, a cousin of some sort. I can't remember how the subject came up, but he was interested when I said that you knew Mr Cross. He said he supposed you were looking for the dirty details of the Venice story; the version he had heard was that your old friend went mad and threw himself into the canal.'

'How long have you known this?'

'For quite a while.'

'And why did you not tell me?'

'I thought it would keep.'

Pondering that, I played with her hair. She leaned out over the balcony. I pulled her back. Frightened.

'So, you believe the story?' she demanded.

'I am not convinced. The sort of thing people make up; malice of the moment, to keep conversation going.'

My publisher was talking about a cheap reprint of my Venice book. I might suggest a small addition. The thought surfaced: I pushed it under at once, looking hard at my wife. Poor Johnnie.

'Don't repeat that story, not to anyone — ever.' And before she could begin to argue with me I said, 'Come back to bed.'